Admiral Darling

Walter John Trowbridge

PublishAmerica
Baltimore

First printing

Softcover 978-1-4626-5061-3
PUBLISHED BY PUBLISHAMERICA, LLLP
www.publishamerica.com
Baltimore

Printed in the United States of America

To my wife,
Asiati Darling,
with love

TO PAULINE & DOC FOR KEEPING ME INFORMED WHAT IS HAPPENING IN THE FALLS!

Love,

Eddie

FOREWORD

This is basically a romantic novel! While it is set within the historical perspective of the demise of the US Navy's Asiatic Fleet from November, 1941, to March 1st, 1942, the tale is largely fictional. Public references were used to provide the historic background, and some specific detailed information was obtained from *The Fleet the Gods Forgot* by Captain W. G. Winslow, US Navy (ret), but this novel deviates from the actual historical realities from both sources in many instances, and the specifics of the novel are purely fictional.

The author served in the US Army during the Korean War and he has no direct experience with Navy life or operation, nor any naval vessels. The portrayal indicated in this novel about the Navy and its ships, other than the general historical background, is fabricated for the sake of the love affair.

Further, except for an occasion reference to the commanding admirals, all the characters in the novel are fictitious and have no reference to the actual officers and men who actually served on any of the ships.

The author has only visited Manila once briefly, but he has lived in Jakarta (Batavia), Indonesia, for three years in the post-war period. He visited many other places in Indonesia, including Bogor, Bandung, and Bali many times, and Surabaya and Cilacap (Tjilatjap) each once. But again, the accounts and description of these cities in the novel are purely fictional or based on post-war experiences.

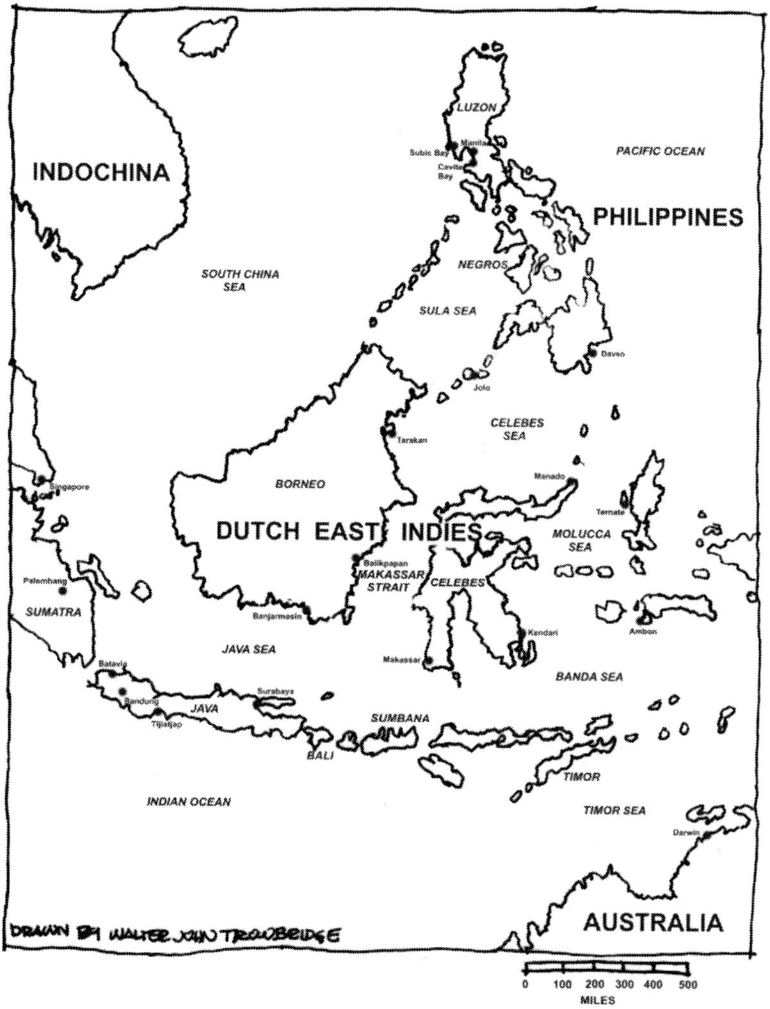

SOUTHWEST PACIFIC ISLANDS

1

Lieutenant Commander William Taylor stepped out of the navy sedan and asked the driver to wait. He walked over to the metal railing, leaned on the top rail, and looked out over the harbor of the Subic Bay Naval Station in the Philippines.

The harbor was filled with ships and it took him some time to find the destroyer USS *Pope*. Indeed, the ship looked the same as so many other destroyers in the harbor, and Bill could only identify the *Pope* by its number, DD-225. While it was an old, almost obsolete, "four-piper" Clemson-class of destroyer dating from just after World War One, it was to be his first command. He was quite thrilled when he finally identified it.

Bill had been selected for this command since he had spent a number of years as the executive officer on another Clemson-class destroyer in the Atlantic Fleet. By now these old ships had been mainly phased out in the Navy. Only the Asiatic Fleet still had a large number of them in service. Indeed, they still had thirteen of these ships left in service.

Actually it was quite lucky that Bill got the command in the first place. It just so happened that no one else was available and qualified to take command of the ship at the precise time someone was required. By sheer coincidence Bill had just recently been promoted and just happened to be on home leave in San Francisco when the need arose. He was immediately given the command of the destroyer and was ordered to depart to Manila as soon as possible. Indeed, the need was so urgent that he was given special permission to fly across the Pacific

Ocean on a civilian Pan American Clipper plane, which took only days rather than a month by boat.

Leaving San Francisco, however, was quite an ordeal. Bill had just broken up with his wife and helped her move with his young son, Billy, into a new apartment off base. She was actually his second wife and she had soured on marriage life, or more likely on Bill himself.

It was similar with his first wife with whom he had three daughters. She hated the military. She had been a very difficult wife and their marriage was thorny right from the beginning. In addition, she liked to flirt with other men, and in the end she was actually having an affair with another man. But that was many years ago.

Bill was a big man, standing six feet two tall and weighing some 210 pounds. He was in his early forties, but still had an athletic body. He had played end on the football team in high school, a forward in basketball, and ran the 440 yard dash in track. But he did not take up sports at the Annapolis Naval Academy, and instead concentrated on being a good navel cadet. He was quite intelligent, and despite fooling around quite a bit in his first year with the girl that became his first wife, he eventually ranked near the top of his class when he graduated.

He was ruggedly good looking, but he certainly was not a “ladies-man”. Indeed, he lacked the “smooth talking” personality that impressed women. Instead, he was somewhat introverted, and was what one might say as being a tall and handsome man, but also a quiet man. While it was true that some women liked him, he was not very good all at "picking up" women or charming them with his wit.

Bill had originally left his three daughters from his first marriage while they were still quite young, varying from six to three years old. But now they were young teenagers. They were sad to see their natural father go, but by now they were used to his not being around much since the divorce some nine years previously. Besides they had a step-father because his first wife remarried right after her divorce was finalized.

But parting with little Billy was different. He was only four years old and did not understand why his father was leaving permanently. He cried when Bill said goodbye and hugged him tightly. Indeed, Bill had to break off his son's embrace in order to catch his flight. It was the saddest thing he ever did, and it really bothered him.

But now Bill was in the Philippines, November, 1941, ready to take command of the destroyer USS *Pope* within the Asiatic Fleet. He climbed back into the naval sedan and bid the driver to proceed to the base headquarters. Even though he was a lieutenant commander, a relatively high level officer, Bill took a long time being processed into his new command. Then he had to make a courtesy call on the base commander, or rather the base's duty officer. He was then shuttled off to the destroyer fleet headquarters, Destroyer Squadron 29, where he had to report to the office of the captain in charge.

Finally, Bill was sent over to the Navy Destroyer Division 59 headquarters, which was the division to which his ship the USS *Pope* was attached.

"Well, well, Billy boy," a familiar voice called out to him.

Bill was surprised to see Philip Towers, an old friend from the Atlantic Fleet days, walk over to him. "I understand you will be joining us," Towers continued with a big smile on his face. And he stretched out his hand in a shake.

"My goodness, Phil," Bill responded merrily as he took Towers hand, noticing the rank on his collar. "Don't tell me that you run the 59th Divison?"

"I certainly do, Bill, have a seat." Phil responded. "And I understand that you are going to be the skipper on one of my destroyers."

"Yes I am, Phil," Bill replied as he sat down in front of Phil's desk.

The two of them then chatted about their time together in the Atlantic Fleet. They had been good friends, and they reminisced about the "old days". Phil was a little older than Bill, and actually outranked him, as he was now a Commander in charge of a fleet division of four destroyers.

Phil did not keep him long, but before Bill left Phil he advised Bill about his executive officer.

"Henry Robertson is a fine naval officer. He is a schooled mechanical engineer and a very sharp one." Then Phil laughed. "He has been in charge of the *Pope* since his predecessor got promoted and was sent back to the States. I think, however, that Henry was hoping to be formally given command of the ship. But actually I don't think he is really "command material". So I am glad that you are aboard."

Phil then directed Bill over to the unmarried officers' quarters, where he was assigned a room.

After freshening up a bit, Bill was anxious to see his ship. He rode in the naval sedan to where the *Pope* was birthed dockside. There was only a skeleton crew abroad the ship at this time, and since Bill's arrival was not yet circulated there was no formal party to greet him.

The officer-of-the-deck was a young officer, Ensign Jim Roberts, who took Bill's salute in a confused manner. Bill explained that he was the new commander of the *Pope* but that he would not be formally taking command until tomorrow. Nevertheless, Bill wanted to have a good at the entire ship beforehand.

"Commander, sir!" another familiar rang out. Bill turned to see Chief Petty Officer Hank Benson saluting him. Bill returned the salute with a big smile.

"Well, Chief," Bill greeted him, "are you on this ship as well?"

"Aye, sir, yes I am" the Chief responded.

Bill knew the Chief also from the Atlantic Fleet. He was a big hulk of a man and the top non-commissioned officer abroad the ship. Bill regarded him as a real top rated sailor. They chatted briefly about their previous time together, but Bill was tired and wanted a quick tour of the ship.

“Sir, the ship is having some refurbishment work done,” Ensign Roberts explained. “It is just some minor work that will be done in a few days.”

“Good, please show me what is being done,” Bill responded.

Then Ensign Roberts and Chief Benson both accompanied Bill through most of the ship, including the current refurbishment work. Having served on a number of these old “four-pipers”, Bill was already familiar with most everything. He thanked them and finally returned to his barracks.

Bill lay down to sleep after his long journey, but he hardy dozed off when he was awaken by loud pounding on his door. It was Albert Hawkins and Richard Rogers, both whom he had also known from their Atlantic Fleet days together. They both were lieutenant commanders, like Bill, and each who had his own destroyer. Al was the captain of the USS *John D. Ford*, Phil’s flagship for the destroyer division, in the same division as Bill’s *Pope*. And Dick was the commander of the USS *Paul Jones*, which was in another destroyer division.

The two of them insisted that Bill join them for some drinks over at the officers club. Despite being jet-lagged Bill could not refuse his old friends, and he went along with them.

Bill met some of his other fellow destroyer commanders, including those in his divisions, plus a number of junior officers. The young Ensign Roberts was also there.

Most importantly, however, he met Lieutenant Henry Robertson, the executive officer of the *Pope* and who was temporarily in charge of the ship. They had a long talk together, and after a few drinks Bill soon learned, as Phil had warned him, that Henry had a secret hope that he would have been assigned as the permanent commander of the *Pope* even though he did not have the proper rank.

Finally, Bill went back to his quarters and had a good night sleep at last. When Bill got dressed the next morning, he had to wear his navy whites for the formal "change of command" ceremony at the ship.

It was ten o'clock when Captain George Warner, the commander of the Destroyer Squadron 29, and Phil, Bill's Destroyer Division 59 commander, came to pick him up. Then together all three of them drove over to the USS *Pope*.

This time all officers and sailors of the *Pope* were assembled on the ship. Captain Warner, Phil, and Bill boarded the ship amid salutes, bulges, and whistles. They were dutifully greeted by Henry as the existing commanding officer. The Captain gave a short speech, followed by Phil, and then they formally turned the ship over to Bill. Then Bill himself gave a "taking command" speech himself. It was a speech that he had prepared long ago in hopes of someday being able to use it when he was given a ship of his own. And now this was that day, and Bill was quite proud.

Henry next formally introduced Bill to all the officers of the ship. Lieutenant Jim Rogers was in charge of damage control, Lieutenant Mike Worthington of weaponry, Lieutenant JG Frank Casanata of the engines, and Lieutenant JG Peter

Lampstich in charge of supply, personnel, and recreation. Under them was another layer of officers, a total of eight in all. And then he was introduced to Chief Petty Officer Benson, whom he already knew, as well as the other petty officers.

After the Captain and Phil departed, Bill was given a formal tour of the ship, including his own cabin, from which Henry had now removed all his possessions. Again, Bill was already familiar with most everything.

Finally the ceremony was over and most of officers and sailors left, leaving only the skeleton crew and a young ensign to remain on board. Bill and Henry lingered on the bridge. Henry, realizing that Bill was a close friend of the Commander, now apologized for his remarks the previous night. He promised Bill that he would be his faithful and dutifully executive officer. Bill thanked him, and said that he knew that Henry was a good officer.

Henry then left and Bill was left alone on the bridge. He sat back on the captain's chair and relished his role as commander of the USS *Pope*. Almost every naval officer waits impatiently over the years for the time when he becomes the captain of his own ship. Since Annapolis, it was the continual dream of Bill to be sitting on the bridge of a ship and being fully in command of all its officers and men.

Bill's time had finally come, and now he had own ship, the USS *Pope*!

He lingered for a while longer and then finally returned to his quarters.

2

Bill spent the next couple of days visiting the *Pope* and checking out the vessel as well as the progress of the refurbishment work. When visiting the engine room or the armaments or whatever, he was accompanied by Henry, Chief Benson, the relevant officer in charge of the section, and the associated chiefs involved. In this manner Bill not only got to know the ship intimately, most which he knew already, but also the crew as well who manned the ship. Indeed, he really was more interested in getting to know the people who operated the *Pope* than the ship itself.

Most of the members of the crew itself were hardy "China" veterans from the time when the *Pope* was stationed in or off China since 1937 during the time when Japan first invaded Manchuria. While Bill was new to the ship, the fact that he had served on a Clemson-class destroyer previously helped him become familiar with the ship as well as earning the respect of the crew. And the good word about him from Chief Benson more or less sealed the crew's opinion.

Several days later Bill requisitioned a vehicle to drive off base in order to do a little sight-seeing in the nearby parts of the Philippines. When he first arrived in the Philippines and was driven from the Clipper port at Manila the fifty miles or so to the Subic Bay Naval Station he was shocked by how crowded the streets and roads were with carts, wagons, animals, and people as well as cars, trucks, and many, many bicycles.

Now he was driving himself as he ventured into the adjacent town of Olongapo. Now he had to actually drive through the crowded streets himself and it was rather nerve racking. He never encountered this amount of congestion before, and he was over-cautious about hitting some thing or someone. He noticed, however, that other cars and trucks just beeped their horns and flowed straight ahead into the crowd.

When Bill ventured out of Olongapo into the countryside the congestion was much less, but people and all sorts of vehicles still wandered about on the road. He also noticed that the adjacent lands consisted of one rice field over another.

As Bill was driving along he soon came upon a fairly elegant limousine stalled by the side of the road, and a matronly Western lady standing next to it. She and the car seemed completely out of place in the Filipino countryside, but Bill noticed that the vehicle had a flat tire. Of course, he stopped to offer his help like a good officer and gentleman.

“May I help you, madam?” Bill asked as he jumped out of his car and approached the lady.

“Oh, thank you, sir” the lady responded politely with a strong European accent. “But my driver and daughter are obtaining some help from the locals.”

Bill introduced himself to the lady, a tall brunette and quite handsome middle aged lady, and she introduced herself as Mrs. Ellen Vanderpan, the wife of an attaché in the Dutch Embassy in Manila. She was quite pleasant and chatted while he examined the tire.

"Oh, this is just a simple job," Bill explained to Mrs. Vanderpan. "It will just take me a few minutes."

With this Bill secured the spare tire and jack out of the trunk. Then while he loosened the flat tire, jacked up the car, and removed the flat, Mrs. Vanderpan continued chatting. She and her daughter were just out for a ride to see this part of the Philippines. She emphasized on how they liked to see the countryside in this different land.

Bill mentioned that he himself had just arrived in the Philippines and it was still all strange to him. He remarked how the streets and roads were such a mess to drive on. Mrs. Vanderpan agreed but said that by now she was quite used to it.

Bill was kneeling on the ground and lifting up the spare tire to mount it on the wheel when he heard a sweet feminine voice behind him.

"Hello, Admiral", came the cheery voice.

Still holding the spare in his hands, Bill turned his head and was shocked to see a most beautiful girl beaming down upon him! She had tossed blonde hair, big blue eyes, and a tremendous smile. He remained frozen in awe of the woman's beauty.

"I brought some help," she continued in a gay voice.

Standing beside her was an elderly Filipino driver who obviously could not change the tire himself, and two young

Filipino boys who they had obviously just been recruited to fix the tire

"Well, ma'am, thank you," Bill finally responded in a flustered voice, "But I am not quite an admiral – yet!"

"That's all right," the girl laughed, "you look so nice in your uniform! Just like an admiral!"

Bill was going to say how beautiful she looked, but he knew that the remark was quite inappropriate, and instead he just shoved the tire onto the wheel studs. Then he stood up, brushing off his hands.

She was tall for a woman, but Bill towered over her. His male eye quickly surveyed her figure and realized that besides being beautiful and jovial, she had a wonderfully shaped body as well – big on top and below and narrow in between.

"I'm Atty Vanderpan, her daughter," the woman introduced herself as she indicated her mother, but without the heavy Dutch accent. Instead she spoke with a slight British accent. She extended her hand out to Bill in greeting. But he turned his hands palms up to show that they were not clean.

"I am sorry, but I don't want to get you dirty," Bill apologized. But she then touched his wrist with her fingers in a greeting, and Bill felt a special thrill pass through his body like a shock wave!

He introduced himself simply as Bill Taylor, a naval officer in the American Navy -- but not yet an admiral.

"Well, it's very nice of you to come to the rescue of two poor stranded ladies," Atty replied.

Meanwhile, the two Filipino boys proceeded to install the nuts on the studs of the wheel to lock on the spare tire, and Bill issued commands to them as if they were his crew on his ship.

"But they don't speak English," the elderly Filipino driver mentioned, and everyone laughed. Nevertheless, the boys seemed to understand exactly what Bill was directing them.

"Yes, you sound just like an admiral," Atty continued gaily.

Then the driver directed the boys in cleaning up and putting the tires and tools away while Bill and Atty chatted for a bit, with Atty doing most of the talking. She was quite a gregarious girl, so full of life, and Bill could not help liking her immensely – not only for her beauty and her figure, but for her bubbling personality as well.

When the car was ready to go again, both Atty and her mother thanked Bill again profusely for his assistance. Atty turned to Bill to bid him goodbye while her mother climbed into the car. She smiled wonderfully and touched his wrist with her fingers again. And again he felt a thrill pass through his entire body.

Bill felt very awkward. She was so beautiful that he did not want her to leave. Then in desperation he blurted out ....

"May I see you again?" Bill immediately regretted saying it. It was such sophomoric remark to say to such a beautiful woman. Undoubtedly, many men continually made "hits" on her.

But Atty took no offense to the question and smile graciously. Yes, she had many men try to make out with her, but she felt this man was different. She liked him. He seemed to be the strong, silent type that she appreciated now after all the years with the other types of men.

Atty then talked to her mother in Dutch. And from their looks it seemed as if they were talking about him. Then she turned back to Bill with a big smile on her face.

"Yes," Atty answered graciously. "Why don't you come to a party we are having at the Dutch Embassy on Saturday night." Her mother then spoke to her in what sounded were a few cross words in Dutch.

Atty, nevertheless, repeated her invitation. When he explained that he had just arrived in the Philippines and had never been in Manila except when the plane landed there, she told him to bring an officer friend who knew the way. But then he pleaded that that he had no civilian clothes.

"Are you trying to avoid my invitation," Atty laughed. "I like men in their pretty uniforms. They make you look so handsome. Be sure to come!"

Then suddenly she reached forward, clasped his wrist in her hand, and very quickly gave him a little kiss on his cheek. Then she drove off with her mother, who obviously disapproved of her daughter's actions.

Bill just stood there dumbfounded as he watched the car disappear down the road.

Needless to say, Bill was quite taken with the beautiful Dutch girl and he could not keep her out of his mind. Not only was she beautiful and had a good figure, but also she was full of life. He kept remembering her lovely face and her gracious manner.

Bill quickly made his way back to the base. His mind was so occupied with thoughts of the girl, however, that he almost ran into an ox cart or something else on the road as he drove to the base.

Back at the base, he thought that this would be a good opportunity to seal his relationship with his executive officer by inviting Henry to come with him to the party at the Dutch Embassy. Since practically all of the American military dependents had already left the Philippines due to the growing hostility with Japan, there were few social occasions left for an American naval officer, other than meeting local girls or just drinking at the bar with the other officers.

When Bill asked him to join him at the Dutch Embassy, Henry was highly pleased with the invitation. He was very excited, and while he did not know where the Dutch Embassy was located, he promised Bill that he definitely would find out.

When Saturday night came around Bill and Henry wore their formal dress white naval uniforms. Henry had lined up a navy sedan to use, and it was he who drove the fifty miles to

Manila. Bill hoped that he could make a good impression with the beautiful Atty.

When Bill and Henry arrived at the Dutch Embassy they were escorted into a large ballroom. There were few females present as most of the dependents of the diplomats had also left Manila as well. And there were only a few military personnel present, all of which were of very senior rank.

Among the American naval military personnel there were a few admirals and captains. Henry pointed out Admiral Hart, commander of the Asiatic Fleet, and Admiral Glassford, commander of Task Force 5. Also Henry identified Captain Warner, commander of Destroyer Squadron 29, which included all thirteen destroyers, and Captain Rooks, commander of the USS *Houston*, which was the flagship of the Fleet.

Bill noticed with a tinge of embarrassment that only he and Henry were of lower rank present at the gathering. And he was particularly disappointed that Atty was not there.

But then suddenly there was quite a commotion when she entered. With her blonde hair, flashing blue eyes, a flowing blue dress, and a bubbling personality, she was a sight that made all male eyes turn toward her. When Bill told Henry that she was the woman who had invited them, Henry seemed frozen speechless and just stared at her in wonderment.

Bill watched Atty as she made her way around the room greeting ambassadors and other senior officials. Slowly she circulated among the guests, seemingly greeting most everyone, and until finally she ended up in front of Bill. Both he and Henry were really stunned by her appearance, and poor Henry was still entirely speechless.

"Welcome to the Netherlands, Admiral," Atty addressed Bill in her usual merry voice. And before he could respond she leaned over and kissed him on his cheek again.

Bill almost stammered his response, and it took him a second or two to recover from the little kiss. Then back to normal, he introduced Henry to Atty. Poor Henry still seemed memorized, but Atty kept up with the banter and soon made both of them feel at ease.

Meanwhile, Atty's mother, Mrs. Vanderpan also arrived and greeted the trio, and Bill introduced Henry to her. She was tall and slim, like Atty, with a good figure like her daughter. Soon even Atty's father arrived and Atty introduced him all around. He was tall and very distinguished looking, just like a diplomat. Bill could see that Atty's good looks came from her parents. Both her parents were polite to Bill, but not very friendly. Indeed, they really did not seem to approve of their daughter's invitation to the American navy officers to the Embassy party.

Atty also had to socialize with the other guests, and she would slip off now and then. Bill felt a little jealous. But he realized that being one of the few women present at the party, it was her duty to circulate among the guests. And she always came back to Bill and Henry.

When the music started Atty insisted that Bill dance with her. While Bill was not a particular good dancer, the music was slow and he was able to handle it all right. And holding Atty in his arms seemed like heaven to Bill. And it was so exciting when occasionally she bumped her lovely body against his, and he could feel her breasts on his chess. She continually chatted as they danced with Bill only adding a word now and then.

But the party finally ended and it was time to go. It was too soon for Bill, but Atty escorted them out to their car. Henry turned to extend his hand to her in goodbye but grasping it she stepped forward a placed a kiss on his cheek – which Henry cherished the rest of the night.

Atty then turned to Bill, and she made no pretense to hold his hand. Instead, she pulled him forward and kissed him right on his lips. Bill felt a thrill pass through his body, and he automatically tried to embrace her in his arms and kiss her passionately. But she laughingly broke away, and simply said good-bye.

Bill paused for a moment as if he was in a stupor. Then as Atty backed away he climbed into the car after Henry. She had a big smile as she waved to them as they drove away, with Henry driving and Bill trying to get a last look at her.

On the way back to the base Bill was silent as he lovingly recalled every moment of the evening, particularly when he held her in his arms dancing and could feel her body against his. And the kiss on his lips lingered with him all the way back to the base. Henry, meanwhile, chattered away almost endlessly. He could not stop talking about Atty, as Bill could not help thinking about her. Indeed, Bill kept trying to think of ways of seeing her again.

The next day, Sunday, Bill called the Embassy and left a message for Atty about meeting her again that day. She soon returned the call and apologized that she was busy that day but said otherwise she was relatively free. With Thanksgiving coming that week, on which he was off duty, Bill asked her whether she would like an American Thanksgiving dinner at the base. She willingly accepted, and she said that she would come in an embassy car.

3

Meanwhile, the refurbishing work on the USS *Pope* was completed, and Bill took out the ship for his initial run and familiarization with the crew. It was the Monday following his meeting with Atty, and he was quite overjoyed with being able to see her again later that week. But now he was thrilled to finally being taking the USS *Pope*, his first command, out to sea.

All the officers and sailors were aboard when Bill arrived at the dockside. He now came aboard as the commanding officer of the fully staffed ship, and after glancing around he went up to the bridge. Henry was waiting for him, as were Lieutenants Rogers and Worthington, his damage control and gunnery officers respectively. Bill directed Henry to proceed to cast off, and Henry gave the commands accordingly.

Bill had done this many times before on the same class of destroyer, but now he was in command and he was the one giving the orders to his executive officer accordingly. Bill was extremely excited as the ship swung away from the dock and moved out into the bay. Soon they headed out of Subic Bay and into the South China Sea.

The USS *Pope* was named after John Pope, a career United States Navy officer in the American Civil War. Born in Sandwich, Massachusetts, in 1798 John Pope was appointed midshipman from Maine in 1816. Prior to the Civil War, he served in the Mediterranean, West Indian, Brazil, African, and East India Squadrons.

From October, 1861, John Pope was attached to the Gulf Squadron commanding Richmond. He participated in the search for CSS Sumter in the West Indies while on his way to join the Gulf Blockading Squadron. He assisted in the blockade of the passes of the Mississippi River and took part in the engagement with Confederate States' vessels at the Head of Passes Battle in October, 1861.

Pope was relieved of his command at his own request on account of ill health. He was later promoted to a commodore in July 1862 and then retired. He died in 1876 in Dorchester, Massachusetts.

In Bill's efforts to become familiar with the ship's crew, he directed the ship in all sorts of maneuvers to see how well the crew responded. In particular, Bill had the crew come to general quarters several times, but they were all old hands and they performed very well. Then Bill practiced various stages of damage control, again to see how the crew responded.

Then there was gunnery practice. First, various air-borne targets were launched and the anti-aircraft crews practiced shutting them down. Then came the gun crew practice to hit targets set out in the water.

And then there was torpedo practice. Since torpedoes were rather expensive, only three of them were used in mock attacks. Unfortunately, none hit the targets, or at least as far that he could tell. Bill would find out later that many of his torpedoes, as well as those in other ships, were actually duds.

Finally there was depth charge launching practice. Again, to conserve on costs only two depth charges were actually launched.

Then the *Pope* sailed back into Subic Bay. Back in the base, Bill had meetings with all the officers and petty officers to discuss the day's practice and suggestions to improve them.

He took the ship out again the Tuesday and Wednesday before Thanksgiving. Over the two days the crew did extremely well in coming to general quarters and in damage control responses. This was a reflection of the crew being well trained veterans. And the gunnery crews did fairly well on both the air-borne and water-borne targets.

The torpedo practice went quite good as well. Using three torpedoes each day, one shot on Tuesday just missed the target, and on Wednesday one actually hit it, but didn't explode. That was one of three, but Bill was concerned about how many torpedoes were actually duds.

Bill was quite satisfied with the crew, and he felt lucky to have well trained old hands. At the same time the officers of the ship and the rest of the crew had the opportunity to assess their new captain, and they all agreed with Chief Benson that he was quite capable. Indeed, they felt very comfortable with Lieutenant Commander William Taylor as being their new commanding officer,

There was no more practice the following day since the next day was Thanksgiving. And Bill had a date with the lovely Atty.

4

On Thanksgiving Day Atty had said that she would be coming with an embassy driver. Bill made arrangements with the front gate to let the embassy car onto the base and to direct it to the officers' mess. And he requested that they let him know whenever the car passed through the gate.

When Bill received the call from the front gate that the embassy car had just gone by, he stood outside the officers' mess and waited patiently for Atty to arrive.

There were a number of men standing around outside the officers' mess, and when Atty stepped out of the car all eyes were on her. Bill extended his hand out to greet her, but she grasped his hand and pulled him towards her and instead gave him a kiss.

All of the men stood there gaping, and some of them politely tipped their caps and watched enviously. And also there were a few low sounding whistles. Atty was quite used to this and simply ignored them and took Bill's arm as they entered the officers' mess.

There were only a few women left on the base as most of them had already departed for the States. There were, however, several women at the officers' mess that day, mainly the wives of the most senior officers, and they were greatly outnumbered by the men.

So needless to say, when Bill entered the officers' mess with Atty, she caused quite a sensation. At first there was an eerie silence as Bill took Atty up to meet the senior officers and the few wives that were present. Atty knew some of them who had attended the party at the Dutch Embassy earlier.

Then many of the officers, particularly the young ones, rushed forward to be introduced. Bill introduced the officers he knew, while Henry and Al Hawkins introduced some others. And finally there were still other officers who introduced themselves.

During the "social hour" before dinner all the "Don Juan" handsome men tried to impress Atty, but she graciously fended them off. Bill was surprised since most girls would be taken in by all the gregarious talk. She was, however, quite used to all this male attention and knew how to handle it quite gracefully. She clung to Bill's arm in a manner to indicate that she was not interested in the other men.

Bill felt quite flattered. After all, he did not have the baby-face handsomest of some of these officers nor the gift of their gab. Yet this beautiful girl clung closely to him all the time.

When dinner was served Atty and Bill were seated at the "admirals' table", undoubtedly because of Atty. Two admirals Bill did not know, their two wives, Captain Warner, Captain Rooks, and another captain or two were all present. Bill was the only lowly officer at the table. Atty had met most of the senior officers before.

Atty herself was quite gregarious, and she and the two admirals' wives got along wonderfully as they chatted about women things. But Atty was also quite good with the men as well. Indeed, it seemed that she was able to socially intermix with just about most anyone. She certainly made the whole table quite joyous.

Needless to say, Atty made Bill quite famous, or infamous as the case may be, among his fellow officers. And, indeed, they were all jealous of him, which embarrassed Bill somewhat.

Finally the Thanksgiving dinner was over and Bill walked Atty back to her car. They agreed to meet again on Sunday, when Atty promised to show Bill around Manila. They agreed that Bill would pick her up at the embassy and then she would show him around town.

Meanwhile, men began crowding around just to look at Atty, so she quickly climbed in the car. Then as Bill bent into the car to say goodbye, she grabbed him around his neck and kissed him. As she rode off Bill was highly elated. The remaining men just looked at Bill in a wondrous manner, and muttered envious comments.

Actually, Bill wondered what Atty saw in him. He did not have the baby-face handsomeness that most women admire, and he was not very good with women. Indeed, he had two failed marriages. In fact, some women considered Bill quite boring since he was essentially the strong, silent type.

Atty, on the other hand, was so attractive and gregarious that seemingly she could have any man she wanted. Bill could not really fathom why she apparently liked him, but time would tell. Meanwhile, he wanted to be with her as much as he could.

For two days afterwards Bill took the *Pope* on patrol duty with the rest of Phil Tower's Destroyer Division outside of Manila Bay. But on Sunday he was free, and he drove alone to the Dutch Embassy in Manila. Again, it was torturous driving but at least he remembered the way Henry had taken them the other night.

Atty was waiting for him at the embassy entrance as he drove up. She was glad to see him and even gave him a warm kiss. Then she directed him around town to see some of the sights. The drive along Manila Bay itself was quite pretty, with its harbor full of ships.

The first stop was at the Cathedral of Manila. It was a lovely church dating from way back to the sixteenth century. It was filled with ornaments, furniture, statues, and images of remarkable antiquity and beauty. It had several chapels dedicated to different saints.

Atty and Bill also stopped at several museums. The Bahay Tsinoy, one of Manila's most prominent museums, documented Chinese lives and contributions in the history of the Philippines. The Metropolitan Museum of Manila exhibited Filipino arts and culture. And the Museum of Manila is the city-owned museum that exhibits the city's culture and history.

Next, Atty directed Bill to a nice restaurant on Manila Bay where they had an early dinner. They spent a long time together at the dinner, and then afterwards, they lingered as they chatted about themselves.

Bill mentioned his two difficult marriages, his three daughters, and his father-less son. He explained that technically he was still married since his second wife had not yet filed for divorce.

Bill had met his first wife when he first attended the Annapolis Naval Academy. She came from a wealthy family in Boston and was there in Annapolis in some sort of women's auxiliary organization, but she dropped out after a couple of years. She was eager to get married, however, and they did so after Bill graduated, despite the objections of both parents. Indeed, both of them were quite young at the time.

But their marriage started off badly and remained sour over the years. She wanted Bill to leave the Navy and take up a more fruitful profession, but Bill refused. During his long absences at sea, thereafter, she started fooling around with other men. The only thing that kept them together was the children. In fact, they separated for a while and it was only the potential arrival of a third child that brought them back together again. While the marriage lasted for a few years longer, it soon became quite meaningless. Bill's wife began fooling around with other men again, and finally even began to have an affair with one of them. That finally ended the marriage.

After Bill left, the other man moved in with Bill's wife and they were married when the divorce was final. The other man essentially raised Bill's daughters, who were still young when he left. Bill remained close to his daughters, or as close as he could being a naval officer and often away at sea. Nevertheless, he saw them every week when he was home and wrote them at least once a month when he was not.

The second marriage was much better. The love for Bill by his second wife lasted much longer. Ironically, she was the opposite from his first wife. She came from a poor family and was not well educated, although she was quite sharp. But then suddenly after their first child, his son little Billy, she changed radically. Her love died out and she became quite weird. For the sake of his own sanity Bill had no choice but to walk out of this strange marriage as well, leaving poor Billy fatherless.

Atty also had an experience with a bad marriage. She too married young, also against her parent's approval, and she was also divorced. Her husband had been one of those baby-faced smooth talkers like the young men in the officer's club. But she soon discovered that he was "all talk and no do" – a common trait of those kinds of men. That is why she now liked somebody stronger and more stable, like Bill.

Atty left her husband even though she was pregnant at the time, and formally changed back to her maiden name. She now had a young son a little older that Bill's son, Billy. Presently, he was back in Holland being cared for by her sister.

Atty had come to Batavia, the Dutch capital in the Netherlands East Indies, on a vacation to visit her parents. But she could not go back when Germany invaded Holland over a year and-a-half ago, and she was stuck in the East. She was eager to see her son again but she could not go a back until after the war. More recently she had followed her parents to Manila when her father was transferred here some nine months ago. Now Atty was about thirty years old, some ten years younger than Bill.

The two of them had quite a pleasant time. They found that they had a lot in common despite the differences in nationalities and personalities. Atty liked to travel and had been all over Europe and even made a trip to America, visiting New York, Chicago, and San Francisco, places that Bill had visited many times. But this was her first time in Asia. In his Navy career Bill had been all over the world, but being in the navy he was limited in what he actually could see and do.

Atty read a lot and could speak different languages, including French, German, and English, as well as Dutch of course. Since coming to the Philippines she picked up some Tagalog. While staying in Bavaria, she picked up several Indonesians languages, Sudanese from West Java and Bahasa Indonesian, the more "national language" spoken in the mixed cultural environment of Batavia, the capital of the colony.

Bill, on the other hand, confessed that he could only speak English. He admitted that he first came from a part of the States where Dutch migrants had settled in the last century. The older generation even still spoke Dutch, but he did not learn a word of it. He remarked the most of the Dutch settlers were farmers and had many little small villages like Oostburg near where Bill lived. There was even a village named Batavia that contained only several hundred people.

Atty thought this was quite funny – a little village in America with the same name as the capital the Dutch East Indies with over half a million people. Bill mentioned that these American-Dutch, particularly the farmers, were very strict Dutch Reformed Church members who didn't drink, smoke, dance, or gamble, and they did not mix with other non-Dutch peoples.

Atty laughed again. This contrasted with the Netherlands today she mentioned. While the Dutch Reformed Church, an offshoot of Calvinism, was still prominent in Holland today, so were Catholics. And Holland had a long history of religious toleration, while religious freedom was now contained in its constitution. Indeed, this is where the Pilgrims came first from England to get away from religious prosecution in England before they went to America.

In due course, their lengthy dinner came to end, with each of them knowing the other much better now. Bill drove Atty back to embassy. After he let her out of the car, Atty embraced him and kissed him for several minutes. He felt quite a thrill with her kiss – and the pressure of her female body pressed against his.

"You're really quite nice," Atty whispered to Bill, "and I think I love you!" Before he could respond she dashed away and headed back into the embassy.

All Bill could think as he watch her disappeared was …. "Yes, and I adore you!"

On his way back to the base, Bill was overwhelmed with joy. He could not stop thinking about her. She was beautiful, jovial, and so wonderful to be with. And she apparently liked him very much. Whether she really loved him might be asking too much, but he certainly wished that it was true.

He could not wait to see her again.

5

On the very next day, Monday, December 1st, Bill was called into the Destroyer Squadron 29 headquarters together with all thirteen of the destroyer skippers and the Division commanders. The startling news was that because of the worsening political situation with Japan and the increasing possibility of hostilities, Admiral Hart had ordered that most of the surface warships of the Asiatic Fleet would be dispersed to the south.

The heavy cruiser USS *Houston,* the flagship of Task Force 5, was being sent to Iloilo, on the island of Panay, in the southern Philippines. It was to be joined later by Admiral Glassford, the commander of the Task Force. The *Boise*, the newly acquired light cruiser commandeered from convoy duty from the States, was being redeployed to Cebu, also in the southern Philippines.

The more obsolete light cruiser *Marblehead,* meanwhile, was being sent to Tarakan, in northeast Borneo in the Netherlands East Indies. It was to be escorted by the destroyer *Paul Jones*, the flagship of Captain Warner, commander of Destroyer Squadron 29, as well as the four destroyers of Destroyer Division 58 and the destroyer tender *Black Hawk.* Destroyer Division 57, on the other hand, was being redeployed to Balikpapan, farther south on the east coast of Borneo.

Finally, Destroyer Division 59, Bill's division, was to be left behind to patrol outside of Manila Bay. After this general meeting, Commander Phil Towers called another meeting with just his four destroyer skippers, including Bill. Phil laid down the patrol schedule with all four destroyers patrolling during daylight hours, and then two destroyers taking turns at night. Bill's nighttime partner was Phil's division flagship, the USS *John D. Ford*, commanded by Bill's friend Al Hawkins.

Bill was quite glad to be remaining in Subic Bay and Manila. This would give him a chance to see Atty again, and to continue their little romance. But getting away to meet her would prove difficult since he was "on-duty" most of the time.

After stocking up on supplies and fuel, all various ships departed the very next day. Bill watched the USS *Houston* steam out of the bay and then the *Boise*. Next came the *Marblehead* escorted by the five destroyers of Division 58 and the tender *Black Hawk* on its way to Tarakan. Finally the four destroyers of Division 57 headed out for Balikpapan.

Bill already knew Phil Towers, commander of Destroyer Division 59, and Albert Hawkins, skipper of the flagship *John D. Paul* from their Atlantic Fleet days. Since arriving in Subic Bay he also met the captains of the other two destroyers, Harry Keith of the *Peary* and George Pound of the *Pillsbury*. These four destroyers followed the other ships out of Subic Bay and took up their designated positions on patrol outside of Manila Bay.

At least, Bill thought, remaining behind in the northern Philippines left him closer to the new love of his life. Now if he could only get into Manila itself.

This assignment continued most of the week, patrolling every day and every other at night. Meanwhile he and his ship, together with the other three destroyers were still based in Subic Bay – some fifty miles away from Manila and from Atty. There was no way he could get off to see her.

Then near the beginning of the day on Thursday, tragedy struck. The four destroyers just happened to be in close formation with the flagship *John D. Paul* off the *Pope's* port bow, the *Pillsbury* to the starboard, and the *Geary* beyond. Then a command came from the flagship to swing sharply to the starboard. .

George Pound, the normal skippered of the *Pillsbury*, just happened to be on sick leave that day and the ship was being sailed by a junior officer. For some unknown reason this junior officer did not respond to the command and continued straight away. As a horrible consequence the bow of the *Pillsbury* plowed into the starboard side of the *Pope* just behind the bow!

The collision sent shock waves through the ship and almost knocked Bill out of his chair. He brought the ship to a halt, and signaled Phil about the collision. He sent Lieutenant Rogers, the damage control officer, down to impact area to assess the damage. Henry also went along. They soon reported that a large gaping hole had been ripped in the hull, fortunately above the waterline, and in addition some damage was done to the interior of the ship behind the bow.

Apparently, the *Pillsbury* suffered only a slightly damaged bow, but Phil signaled both ships to retire to the Cavite Bay Naval Yard inside Manila Bay for repair. According, the *Pope* limped back into Manila Bay and to the Navy Yard at Cavite

Bay, with the *Pillsbury* following. Both ships were laid up for repair.

Bill was highly embarrassed by the collision, even though it was not his fault. He had just taken command of the ship just weeks before, and he already had a collision with another destroyer. He felt just terrible.

An inquest soon followed. Bill was absolved of any wrong doing, but the poor Lieutenant JG was relieved of his duties aboard the *Pillsbury.* And George Pound was livid as to what had been done to his ship.

Both Bill and Henry were occupied with the repair of the *Pope* in Cavite Bay Navy Yard. Henry took the lead since he was a mechanical engineer and was good at these sort of things, while Bill organized the logistics to get the repair work done. At the same time work was also proceeding on the repair of the *Pillsbury's* bow in the next wharf.

While Bill was quite busy in the repair work of his ship, this gave him some opportunity to take off Sunday to see Atty. Indeed, at Cavite Bay he was less than ten miles away from her. He called Atty and he scheduled to see her Sunday morning. She suggested that they go swimming together and then have dinner at her house. Bill though that would be great. She would bring the towels, a big blanket, and a picnic lunch, and she reminded him to bring along his swimming suit.

Then Atty gave Bill directions on how to get to her house. It was very complicated, but Bill was a good navigator – on land as well as at sea – and he felt sure that he could find his way there.

It was still a week before the Pope would be ready to be seaworthy again, and Henry was supervising all the work. That evening he told Henry what he planned to do, and gave him the same directions where he would he could be reached. He intended to be back Sunday night, or maybe even early Monday morning at the latest.

Henry laughed, but assured Bill that if he had a girl like Atty living nearby he too would be off in a flash to see her. Indeed, Bill was now less than ten miles away from his love.

6

It was the morning of Sunday, December 7th, in the Philippines when Bill drove up to Manila to pick up Atty from her house, which was not far from the Cavite Bay Navy Yard.

Bill was not familiar with the crazy streets of Manila and together with them being crowded with every form of transportation, animals, and people, he had a hard time finding Atty's house. But being a good navigator he finally was successful, even though he was late getting there. It was quite a nice house in a rich section of the city as befitting a European government dependent. He approached the door, but Atty came out to greet him before he reached it.

She was dressed in casual clothes this time. Bill could not help noticing that her rather tight sweater, even wearing it somewhat it loosely, really showed off her breasts very well. Her thin waist and flaring hips really gave her a very pronounced "hourglass" figure. Bill was stunned by her appearance, but pleasantly so, but he was careful not be ungentlemanly and stare at her.

"Well, Admiral, I hope that you are better at sailing your little boat than driving in Manila," Atty laughed. And she did not hesitate to embrace Bill and give me a nice kiss! Again he felt a great thrill pass through his body as she pressed her lovely female form against his body.

"I hope so too," is all Bill could say with a laugh. Then he followed her back into the house.

While waiting for Atty to gather up her belongings, he noticed that the interior of the house was as elegant as its exterior. It was nice, he mused, to be a European, or a civilian American for that matter, in a poor country like the Philippines.

Soon Atty arrived back with a little basket, for snacks as she explained, topped with her suit, towels for both, and a big blanket. She handed them to Bill to carry, and together they walked out to Bill's navy car.

Atty directed him out of the city as he fought the mixed traffic, passed Cavite Bay, and headed southward along the coast. She said that she knew a spot where there would not be too many people, even on a weekend. When they arrived at the selected coast still within Manila Bay, Bill parked the car. He noticed that hardly anyone else was there as Atty had promised.

Atty, meanwhile, summoned two little Filipino boys to show them a good spot where they could change into their swim suits, and carry the gear for them. She spoke to them in Tagalog, and Bill was quite impressed with her knowledge of languages.

They passed into a thicket of trees which provided them good cover to change into their swimming suits. Bill stared at Atty as she started to pull up her sweater, but she halted as she looked disapprovingly at him.

"Well, turn around, Silly," Atty scolded him. "Please be a gentleman and give me some privacy."

Obediently, Bill turned around like a gentleman. But he noticed that Atty did not say anything to the two little boys. They just stood there staring at the woman as Bill turned around, and he knew that despite their young age they relished the idea of seeing a naked female – particularly a beautiful and sexy one like Atty. But he knew that European women, particularly Dutch women, were quite casual about such things.

"All right now, you may turn around now," Atty finally announced.

When Bill turned back around, he was delighted with the sight of Atty in her swimming suit. It was a one piece outfit that fit tightly to her body, and showed off her figure just wonderfully. Indeed, her breasts were quite pronounced in the thin garment.

"All right, Admiral, close your mouth," Atty laughed at him. He was quite embarrassed being caught staring at her mindlessly like some sort of school boy.

Then Atty and boys headed to beach while Bill changed into his suit. When he finished he went down to the beach as well. Atty already had the blanket spread out on the sand, had the lunch basket and towels laid out on the blanket, and was dismissing the two young boys with tips. There were only a few other people on the beach, but they were quite far away.

"How about a swim?" Bill volunteered, and Atty nodded in agreement. Hand in hand they walked into the surf, and when the cold water splashed on Atty's upper body she instinctively flung herself against Bill. He certainly did not object to the feel of her thinly-clad female body against his and her breasts pressing on his naked chest.

But then Atty dove fully into the water and began to swim away. She was a good swimmer, but Bill was even better. He soon caught up to her and then with the water neck high, he embraced her in his arms and kissed her on the mouth.

"Stop that," Atty laughed, "people can see us!"

"But there is no one around for a hundred yards," Bill objected.

Atty, however, broke loose and laughingly swam away. Bill quickly caught her again, embraced her, and kissed her again.

"See, every time I catch you I get to kiss you!" Bill insisted.

Atty just laughed and tried to break away again. But this time Bill held her firmly in his arms and would not let her go. In the neck deep water Bill held her tightly against his body and his hands began to play around a little bit! .

"Behave yourself, officer," Atty chided him, and she finally broke away again. Bill quickly swam after her.

They played this little "game" for some time until Atty finally allowed him to embrace her, and give her a nice kiss while she passionately kissed him back. Finally, the two of them walked out of the water, holding each other's hands, until they reached their blanket.

After drying themselves off, Atty and Bill sat on the blanket and had the little snack that she had prepared, including a bottle of wine. They chatted and giggled as they ate and drank the wine. Finally, Bill lay out in the sand, and, since he was awake most of the night before, he quickly dozed off.

Atty took advantage of this to slowly and carefully pour sand on Bill's body until he was completely buried in sand. When he woke up, Bill was surprised that at first he could not move.

"You're my prisoner, Admiral," Atty proclaimed with a giggle. "And I can do with you what I want!" To prove her point she began twisting his ears and then pinching his nose closed.

This last "torture", however, made Bill to make every effort to break out of the sand, which he quickly managed to do. Then he laughingly grabbed Atty and threw her down flat on her back on the sand and rolled right on top of her.

"Now you're my prisoner!" Bill exclaimed as he felt the thrill of laying on top of her female body!

"Admiral Taylor, behave yourself!" Atty complained sharply. "This is unbecoming of an officer of the United States Navy!"

Realizing that he was in a rather obscene spot, Bill quickly rolled off the top of her – as if giving up a pleasurable position.

"That's better, Admiral," Atty now continued more humorously. "All sailors have to learn how to take orders."

"Yes, ma'am!" Bill responded obediently.

Atty then rose up and made another dash into the water, with Bill following close behind her! This time they did not play “mouse and cat” again like before, but they did a lot of embracing and kissing. Bill was a little naughtier with his hand this, trying to grab Atty where he shouldn’t. But Atty was sure to make him behave.

Finally they emerged from the water again and lay down on the blanket again to take a little sun. They lay side by side in a semi-embrace and chatted for a long time, while kissing now and then. As the sun started sinking in the western sky, however, they finally decided it was time to go.

They left their swim suits on and just put on their shirt and sweater. With the Filipino boys gone, this time Bill had to carry everything himself back to the car. Then they drove back to Manila and wound through the streets amid all its congestion just as the sun was beginning to set.

Bill followed Atty into her house, and then after dropping off the basket on the dining table, he followed her into her bedroom. Atty directed him where to place her clothes, the towels, and blanket! Then she started to pull off her sweater, but stopped.

“Turn around please,” Atty directed Bill.

“Yes, ma’am,” he responded and obediently he complied like a proper gentleman.

When Bill turned around, however, he noticed that there was a full length mirror slightly to one side that stood at an angle. He was pleasantly surprised that it actually reflected Atty as she pulled off her sweater, and then began to unzip her swimming suit in the back. She did not notice that Bill could see her.

Bill knew as a gentleman and an officer he should look away – but as a red-blooded male he could not avert his eyes to a beautiful and sexy woman undressing!

When Atty lowered the top of her suit Bill's heart almost stopped as her bare breasts flopped into sight! Her large nipples stuck out big and hard in the cool air of the bedroom! Then she pulled the suit down over her hips exposing her pelvis! Bill could readily see that she was a natural blonde!

Atty bent over to remove the swim suit off her feet and then stood up. She was now completely nude and Bill could hardly breathe as he beheld her fully naked female body!

Then as Atty looked up and she just happened to see that Bill was staring at her reflection in the mirror!

"Shame on you, you naughty Admiral!" she said scoldingly.

But Atty made no effort to cover herself! Instead, she just turned and walked directly over to Bill whose back was turned to her!

"You are not an officer and gentleman," Atty continued as she grabbed hold of Bill from behind and pressed her naked body against his back!

Bill was quite embarrassed, being caught like some sort of peeping Tom. He remained absolutely motionless as Atty hugged him. Then she began to unbutton his shirt and pull it down and off his back!

"And I am going to have a report you to the US Navy!" she continued. Then shockingly Atty pulled down his swim trucks and off his feet! They now were both fully naked!

"Now stand at attention when I am talking to you, sailor!" She continued as she pressed her naked female body against the backside of his naked male body! Bill was thrilled with the feel of her naked flesh against his! And his body was not the only thing "at attention"!

"Yes, Ma'am!," he remained motionless as she rubbed her breasts against his bare back and her pelvis against his naked buttocks!

"Now get ready for inspection, sailor!" Atty intoned. Then she reached her hand around in front of him and took a firm grip on his fully erected sexual organ!

But poor Bill was so overwhelmed by the sexual stimulation that he quickly swung around and embraced the naked Atty front to front!

He was overcome with lustful desire as he felt her naked body against his. Her breasts pressed against his chest and her pelvis pushed his hardened sexual organ to his abdomen. And he rubbed his body against hers as they had a long passionate kiss.

Then Bill picked Atty up in his arms and carried her over to the bed. She did not resist as he laid her out on her back flat on the bed and even spread her legs far apart! She did not object as he knelt between her stretched legs and looked down at her fully exposed womanhood!

Indeed, Atty smiled slightly as she raised her arms way above her head, provocatively thrusting her breasts up toward him! She did not move at all as he automatically reached down with both hands, grabbed her breasts in either hand, and slowly but lustfully began to massage them!

"This is not the proper conduct for an officer of the United States Navy!" Atty mischievously complained to Bill, but she made no effort to stop him!

"Yes, Ma'am, I know it's not," Bill replied with a slight laugh, "but it is certainly fun!"

With this Bill lowered his head down between her breasts and mashed them together with his hands! Again, Atty made no effort to stop him.

"Behave yourself," she continued to complain, "or I will give you a bust in the mouth!"

Almost automatically Bill shifted his mouth to one of Atty's big, hard nipples and sucked on it hungrily! He sucked on one nipple and then the other while all the time Atty remained motionless, but laughingly she threatened all sorts of actions against him.

"I will have you know that this conduct is unbecoming of the US Navy officer and I am going to report you to your superior commander!" Atty continued playfully threatening him but offered no resistance at all!

Bill then lay atop of her body, balancing his weight on his knees and elbows, and rubbed his naked male body on her naked female body! He loved the feel of her breasts against his chest! Then he pressed his lips to hers, silencing her continuing complaints!

Finally, Bill inserted his male sexual organ fully into Atty's body! She did not object!

Bill once again placed his lips on hers, and he proceeded to make love to her! She responded like a passionate woman!

Bill tried to prolong the sexual intercourse as long as possible in order to please the beautiful girl as well as himself. But he reached a point when he could not hold back any longer, and he began to make love to her fast and hard. Atty responded in kind, and it seemed that she had reached fulfillment about the same time as Bill.

Then they both collapsed in sexual exhaustion and satisfaction. Bill rolled off Atty's body and they lay side by side in each other's arms! They lay there for almost an hour before Atty started stirring.

"Dinner time, my darling admiral," Atty coaxed, and she rose out of the bed, put on a dressing gown, and left the bedroom. Bill felt so relaxed and satisfied, and he got up only so slowly. He put on his shorts and pants and a shirt, and also headed out of the room.

When Bill arrived in the dining room, Atty was setting the candle-lite table for two.

"Well good morning, dear," Atty said cheerfully, "did you have fun in bed?"

They both laughed and Bill approached her, gave her a kiss, and slapped her buttocks affectionately.

"Don't be naughty," Atty responded, and then went out into the kitchen. Bill sat down at the table and poured both of them some wine from the bottle Atty had already opened. She returned with some food, and when she was all settled, Bill raised his glass in a toast.

"Here's to our love!" Bill offered. But he was surprised when there was a look of concern flashed on Atty's face momentarily. But then she smiled brightly as she lifted her glass to the toast as well.

"Yes, here's to our love!" she responded. Then they proceeded to eat the simple supper Atty had arranged with her servants to prepare. They chatted merrily as they ate, held hands, and even kissed a little. Towards the end of the meal, after a few glasses of wine, Atty seemed to have a concerned look on her face. But then it quickly passed and instead she asked him to tell her something about himself.

Bill related that he moved to San Francisco with his parents when he was still a child and they lived on Russian Hill in an elegant house with a beautiful view out over the San Francisco Bay, Alcatraz, and Angle Island in the distance. He confessed that he always had a calling for the sea since his parents were well-to-do, and belonged to the San Francisco Yacht Club over in Belvedere. They had nice big sailboats which they often took out onto the San Francisco Bay and out into the Pacific Ocean with Bill and friends. He grew up with the sound of the sails slapping in the wind and the boat swishing through the water, and he just loved it.

Atty said that she too was "drawn" to the water, but she laughed when she admitted it was the water in all the canals in Amsterdam. These canals were the best way to get around the city. Bill replied that he had once visited Amsterdam, courtesy of the US Navy, but he did not see much.

"What about your girl friends?" Atty asked.

Bill ignored the question and instead mention about he used to sit on the balcony of his parent's house and watch the ships sailing into the harbor. He used to keep track of every ship that came into San Francisco Bay and every ship that went out.

"But, what about your girl friends?" Atty asked again, reflecting a more female interest.

"Well, I never really had any," Bill finally answered. "Some girls liked me, but I wasn't interested in them. The ones I did like weren't interested in me. So I never really had a steady girl friend."

Then Bill continued by mentioning that he always wanted to be naval officer all his life. His parents did not approve of it, but his father finally helped him to get an appointment to the Annapolis Naval Academy. He then sadly related that his father died while he was still in school. His mother died years later but she never got along with either of his two wives.

"Of course not," Atty laughed. "Mothers don't like daughters-in-laws. They feel that no woman is good enough for their sons."

"Well, how about you?" Bill asked Atty.

Atty then related something of her childhood. She was raised in Amsterdam amid diplomatic circles and been abroad quite often. She was in school a long time in London when her parents were elsewhere, and that is where she learned her English so well. And that is where she picked up a British accent.

"How about boys?" Bill countered with a query of his own.

Atty giggled and admitted as a young girl she liked to flirt with the boys but nothing serious. She was close friends with a group of girls with a similar background, and like all young pretty girls they had glorious fun with the boys.

Bill suspected that with her looks, Atty probably had many boys after her. Indeed, she admitted that she was a little wild, and had many boyfriends but she was always a step ahead of them. Later, many boys asked her to marry them, and she finally agreed to marry the guy that became her husband because he was so handsome and was so much fun. She married him against the objections and will of her parents.

Indeed, she had already completed three years of Humanities study in the University of Amsterdam, and dropped out to marry him. This was another reason her parents were against the marriage.

It was only after they got married that she realized that her parents were right. It was a big mistake. Despite his great personality her husband really was quite hallow. Indeed, he really had never grown up.

Then when she became aware that she was pregnant her whole attitude changed. From a silly school girl she became a serious woman. Finally she got a divorce from her "empty" husband. Since then she wanted something much different in a man – strength and stability.

Then Atty leaned over gave Bill a kiss. But then suddenly, she seemed to have a concerned look on her face again.

"There is something I must tell you ….," she said hesitantly but then stopped.

"What ….?" Bill responded questioningly. But then that funny look of her face disappeared and she was her merry self again.

"Oh, nothing!" Atty concluded! Then lifting up her glass again and she quickly changed the subject, "let's go make love!"

While Bill was concerned about what was bothering her, he certainly was not going to turn down the invitation to make love to a beautiful girl.

When Atty got up from the table, Bill rushed over and hugged her tightly, and then kissed her. They quickly went arm in arm to the bedroom, their clothes were discarded, and they flung themselves naked on the bed.

They rolled around on the bed together, rubbing their naked bodies on each other. Finally Bill positioned himself on top, and proceeded to make love to her again!

The two of them achieved another wonderful sexual experience, and they fell exhausted and satisfied in each other's arms. Then they went to sleep as they cuddled together.

Bill had made a mental note to himself to get up early so he could arrive back at the ship by dawn.

7

Both of them, however, were awakened much earlier by loud and urgent knocking on the front door of Atty's house! Bill noticed that it was four o'clock in the morning!

Atty quickly put on a dressing robe had headed to the front door with Bill following right after her. Then she opened the door to find Ensign Roberts standing there, highly excited.

"The Japanese have just bombed Pearl Harbor," Roberts blurted out! "They destroyed much of the Pacific Fleet! We're at war!"

Bill was shocked, even though the chances of hostility with Japan had been increasing, particularly during the last several weeks. But he didn't expect it to really happen.

It certainly was the worse timing with the hostilities starting while his ship was still being repaired. Roberts gave him what little information that he knew about the attack, but it was not much more. Bill told Roberts to head back to the Yard and he would follow in a few minutes after he got dressed.

Bill quickly explained to Atty the significant as to what was happening as he returned to the bedroom and put on the rest of his clothes. Then he gave Atty a passionate embrace and kiss. He told he would call as soon as he could, and then he departed in his navy vehicle.

On the way back to the Cavite Naval Yard, Bill tried imagine what had happened back in Hawaii, but the radio in his car did not have much more information other that the fact that the Japanese had bombed Pearl Harbor and other places in Hawaii. Indeed, when they reached the Yard and their ship, Bill found that the news of the attack on Hawaii was just trickling in!

When more information finally became available, he learned that four battleships were sunk and four others damaged. In addition, some three cruisers and destroyers were sunk or damaged as well as a few other ships. Nearly two hundred aircraft were destroyed, and thousands of men were killed or wounded.

This was a tragic blow to the Pacific Fleet. On the other hand, none of the five aircraft carriers of the Pacific Fleet were at Pearl Harbor at the time.

It was now five o'clock in the morning on December 8th in Manila, and everyone expected a similar attack on Subic Bay Naval Station, and maybe even Cavite Bay Navy Yard, similar to the one on Pearl Harbor. Fortunately, all of the Asiatic Fleet surface warships had already been dispersed far to the south, except for the four destroyers of Destroyer Division 59. And of these, two destroyers, the *John D. Ford* and the *Peary* were based in Subic Bay, and two of them, the *Pope* and the *Pillsbury*, were laid up under repair in the Cavite Bay Navy Yard.

When he reached the ship, Bill's immediate action was to prepare the *Pope* and his crew in case the attack came after sunrise. While the repairs on the *Pillsbury* were nearly complete and might be able to put to sea if necessary, the repairs on the *Pope* were still days away from being finished and be sufficiently seaworthy. Meanwhile, as of now the *Pope* was literally dead in the water.

It was hopeless to try to rig up some sort of camouflage for the ship in such a short time. Instead, in case of an aircraft attack, Bill arranged that the most of the crew would take cover in the aircraft shelters behind the wharves. The only ones that would remain of the ship would be the officers and men manning the aircraft guns and those in damage control. He would remain on the ship but Henry, his second in command, would take cover in the shelter to insure he could take command in case Bill was immobilized.

Meanwhile, Bill tried to hurry up the repair of the ship as fast as it could be done. The members of his crew who were qualified to help were also put to work.

Then as the sun rose everyone seemed to be anxiously peering into the sky waiting for a possible air attack. The Yard was filled with ships under repair or those just docked there. Several ships and PBY planes were anchored just off the Yard. And some ten miles away the harbor off Manila itself was filled with some forty merchant ships, the Navy's submarine tenders, and a host of submarines.

Hour and after hour went by with nothing happening, and everyone began to relax a bit. Indeed, Bill's mind began to shift to Atty and the wonderful time he had with her the previous day and evening.

Then, in the early afternoon, reports came in that the Japanese were bombing the Army Air Corps base at Clark Field and caught most of the American planes on the ground just after the latter had returned from reconnaissance flights. Everyone again started to prepare for an attack on Cavite Bay Navy Yard, but again nothing happened. The afternoon passed into evening and the men returned to the barracks. Bill, however, spent the night on the *Pope*.

The next day, Tuesday, was similar. Everyone waited for an attack early in the morning. When it did not occur by noon, people began to relax more. But reports were received that Japanese planes again attacked Clark Field and more American airplanes were destroyed. It appeared that the Japanese were first concentrating on knocking out the American air forces to permit their own planes to have full freedom of the skies.

The afternoon passed at the Cavite Yard without any incidents.

Then the next morning, Wednesday, December 10th, everyone was back at their stations and repair work continued on the two ships. Actually, work on the *Pillsbury* was now complete and its engines were fired up. The repair of the *Pope*, however, was still a few more days away.

Meanwhile, reports were received that small Japanese army units had made invasion landings at various places far away on the north shore of Luzon. But with nothing happening at Cavite Bay Navy Yard, people began to relax again. Officers and seamen went off to lunch.

But then suddenly at 1245 the air-raid sirens went off!

In accordance to Bill's emergency plans, the *Pope's* crew either headed for shelter or to their assigned positions at damage control stations or anti-aircraft guns. Bill himself remained on the bridge. The various ships that were able to quickly get out of the Navy Ward steamed out into Manila Bay where they could evade aircraft attacks. The *Pillsbury* was one of them. The PBY planes that had crews available also cleared out. And Bill could see in the distance the many submarines that had been near Manila harbor break away from their tenders and head for the deep water of Manila Bay in which to submerge.

About twenty minutes later a host of enemy bombers with fighter escorts arrived over Cavite Bay Navy Yard. The base and the ship's anti-aircraft guns began firing, but the planes remained above 19,000 feet in the sky, out of range for all the guns. The bombers circled the Yard and began bombing whatever they chose, unmolested by gun fire or American planes of which there were none. Soon the Yard itself was exploding as the bombs hit oil tanks, and buildings, and even the docks themselves. Soon everything seemed to be on fire!

During the first two waves of planes bombs burst nearby the *Pope*, lying helpless at its wharf, but they did not damage the ship. But bombs from the third wave hit the wharf and straddled the ship.

Then tragically a bomb hit the *Pope* itself. White-hot shrapnel flew all around, some penetrating the bridge itself.

The helmsman and an ensign on the bridge were killed instantly. Bill was hit in both legs by flying shrapnel and was thrown to the deck. Two other officers on the bridge were wounded as well as several seamen.

Bill blacked out momentarily, but then upon recovering himself he noticed that blood was flowing from both legs, but he felt no pain due the shock of his wounds. He tried to rise up, but Ensign Roberts quickly held him down. Soon a corpsman arrived and gave Bill some painkillers while he temporarily stopped the bleeding in his legs by wrapping them with bandage tape.

The painkillers made Bill drowsy and he really could not follow what happen next. It was only later that he learned that the minesweeper *Whippoorwill* had come to the rescue of the *Pope* and after several attempts managed to tow the stricken ship out of the infernal and out into the relative safely of Manila Bay. The crew of the *Whippoorwill* helped put out the fires on the *Pope,* and helped with the wounded, including bandaging Bill's leg wounds.

In due course, after the enemy planes left, the *Pope* was berthed again, and the dead and wounded were taken off the ship. Even though he was still drugged Bill insisted that all the wounded were removed from the ship before he left.

Bill and the other wounded men were taken to a nearby Navy hospital. He was housed in a two-man room in the officers' section of the hospital. Bill was given more medicine to kill the pain now that the shock had worn off. It continued to dull his brain, and he hardly realized when later in the afternoon he was taken down to radiology to have his legs x-rayed.

Still later, a doctor arrived to give him the good news that most his wounds were minor cuts and that there was only a few pieces of shrapnel in his legs, all near the surface and easily removed. He was scheduled in surgery early the next morning to remove the remaining shrapnel.

That night Bill was still in daze from the medicine. In his mind he continued to hear the explosions of the bombs and visualize the Navy Yard all in flame. He tried, instead, to think of Atty and of they making love, and that provided some mental relief.

Then it was early in the next morning when the Filipino nurses prepared him for surgery and he was moved onto an operating room trolley. The anesthetist arrived to put him to sleep, and then all Bill could remember was rolling down the corridor and the bright lights of the surgery room before he dropped off completely.

8

When Bill began to wake up in the recovery room, his blurred vision could only detect a face that looked like an angel.

“Am I in heaven?” he asked weakly. He lifted his hand toward the angel and unwittingly grasped a woman’s breast.

“Oh, darling, you are awake!” came the angel’s voice.

As Bill began to focus his eyes he realized the angel was really Atty – and that he was holding her breast in his hand. Then she pulled away, and as his eyes began to return to normal he made her out more sharply. Then he also saw Henry standing in back of her.

“My goodness,” Bill exclaimed as his head partially cleared up. “I may not be in heaven, but the next best thing to it!” as he eyed Atty.

“Hello, admiral darling,” she chimed as she sat on his bed, and she gave him a nice kiss. Bill’s hand automatically reached up and grasped her breast again. “Stop that!” she chided him, and she pulled his hand away.

“Well at least he is not dead!” Henry stated with a laugh. ““How are you doing, skipper?” Henry greeted him.

Henry was in the bomb shelter as planned during the attack so he was unscathed from the bombing. He told Bill that he had brought Atty to the hospital since she was in a panic when she leaned that the *Pope* had been hit.

Henry also gave Bill an update on the bombing raid and the current status. He mentioned that besides the ensign on the bridge, one of the ensigns at the guns was also killed in the explosion, and four other officers were wounded, one seriously. Only three officers, including Henry, were not hurt. Eight of the enlisted men had been killed, including the helmsman standing next to Bill, and fifteen had been wounded out of a total of a hundred and twenty-six men. But another fifteen men were missing and they were presumed dead.

With the Cavite Bay Navy Yard itself largely destroyed, and subject to possible more bombings, the *Pope* instead had been taken to a small shipyard in Manila belonging to the Atlantic Gulf and Pacific Company. Their facilities were marginal at best but Henry was directing the boat's crew in the repair work. While he had been told that it would take more than a month to repair, Henry had already started working the crew around the clock in shifts in order to shorten the time.

Soon the doctor arrived while Henry and Atty were both still there in the room. The doctor announced that Bill's wounds were not serious. All the shrapnel had been cleaned out, and he should be up and around in a week or so. Everyone was overjoyed, and Atty gave him a nice big contradictory kiss.

But the doctor warmed that Bill needed to rest after the surgery and suggested that everyone leave. Indeed, he was still on painkilling drugs and still quite dopey. Atty and Henry left, and Bill soon dozed off again.

Later in the day, when he was being fed, he had a chance to talk to his roommate, who had not said anything while Bill's visitors were there. He was a lieutenant who worked in the Navy Yard and had been only slightly wounded in the attack. He expected to be gone within a few days.

Atty came early the next day, and stayed most of the day. Bill was still on some drugs but his mind was clearer now. Atty chatted with Bill or read him some books, or otherwise just sat there while he dozed off and on. She even fed him at his lunch even though he was quite capable of feeding himself. Admittedly, Bill did mind the special treatment he received from a beautiful girl, and his roommate was quite jealous.

The commander of the *Whippoorwill* also came in to see how he was doing after the rescue. Bill thanked him hardily for his bravery in towing the *Pope* out of harm's way, and saving him and his crew in the process. The gallant skipper was quite modest about his bravery under fire.

Phil, his friend and commander of Destroyer Division 59, also came to see Bill. He was glad to hear that he would be recovering soon, before the *Pope* was repaired. He mentioned that Subic Bay Navy Station was also attacked the day before and a lot of navy planes were destroyed. Most of the remaining Asiatic Fleet had left the naval station, and now he and the Division destroyers, less the *Pope*, would be leaving that night for the Dutch East Indies. Bill wished Phil and Bill's fellow commanders good speed, and he hoped to join them soon.

And finally an admiral from the Asiatic Fleet Headquarters came to visit Bill. He congratulated Bill in saving the Pope and it crew. Bill advised him, however, that it was the commander of the *Whippoorwill* that saved the ship and the men, and recommended that he should get a metal for it.

The following day, Saturday, December 13th, Atty came again. This time she helped Bill get some exercise by helping him walk around the hospital. During the next few days he was getting better all the time, and she continued to exercise him, including taking walks outdoors. They spent most of the time in his hospital room as Bill still needed time to recover.

Henry also came daily to report on the repair progress on their ship. It was progressing well and Henry hoped to have it completed by Christmas. But he also reported that Japanese soldiers had also landed in southern Luzon unopposed, and the small units of the Japanese army in the north were moving southward.

Bill's roommate in the hospital was released the following Wednesday, and Bill was now alone in his room. When Atty came that day she said that she could not stay long, but wanted to do "something special" for Bill.

Standing beside the bed, away from the door, Atty opened her blouse and exposed big bra-less breasts to his view! Needless, to say Bill was quite excited about seeing her naked breasts but she told him to just lie back. She then slipped her hand under Bill's covers and grasped hold of his male organ in her hand, which by now was nice and hard.

"Now just relax," Atty giggled as she leaned over Bill and lowered her breasts into his face. Then she shoved one nipple into his mouth which her sucked vigorously. While keeping a wary eye on the door, Atty proceeded to masturbate Bill's male organ at the same time.

Atty switched nipples in Bill's mouth and he sucked on it lustfully! For him it was like being in heaven like he felt when he first woke up in the hospital! He kept sucking her nipples, one after the other, while Atty kept masturbating his hardened organ! It wasn't long before he felt himself reaching a climax, and his whole body became tense! Then he had an orgasm!

Bill fell back on the bed in sexual exhaustion. Atty covered him up with the blanket and discreetly covered herself. Then she gave Bill a nice long kiss.

Atty explained that she would not be coming to the hospital the next day since she had to pack. The Dutch were closing down their Manila Embassy since Japanese soldiers were now in the northern and southern sections of Luzon, and Manila might be bombed soon. Most of the staff, including her, was flying out Friday night to Batavia, the capital of the Dutch East Indies.

Bill was disappointed that Atty was leaving him permanently! By now he was deeply in love with her, and he was concerned that he would never see her again. She said she would be back to the hospital Friday before she flew out. Then she gave him another kiss, patted his bedcovers at his sexual organ, and then left.

Henry now was about Bill's only visitor. The other destroyers in the Division had left days ago and the *Pope* was the only American surface warship left in Filipino waters. Henry said the repair work would take another week at least, even working around the clock on it. Fortunately, Bill should be out of the hospital by then and in command of his ship again. Meanwhile, Naval Headquarters had replaced most of his dead or badly wounded officers and men by now.

On Friday, Atty returned as promised before she flew out that night. She was dressed in an unusual one-piece dress like a slicker! She walked with Bill in his usual daily exercise.

After they returned to the room and Bill lay down on his bed, Atty took a chair and levered it under the handle of the door to prevent it being opened! She then stood next to the bed and pulled the covers off of Bill and opened his hospital gown! Then she quickly unsnapped her slicker dress and set it aside. Bill was surprised, pleasantly so, to see that she was completely naked underneath except for her panties.

Atty then pulled off her panties and threw them on the bed as she climbed in right on top of Bill! She pressed her breasts to his head, and whipped his face back and forth with her dangling lobes. Then she allowed him to suck first one big hard nipple and then the other!

Needless to say, Bill's manhood was now as hard as a rock and standing straight up in the air. Atty shifted so that her female organ hovered over his male organ! Then she grasped the big shaft in her hand and guided it into her body! She quickly lowered her pelvis and took his complete manhood into her body!

Bill tried to move but Atty told him just to lie still! Then she lay fully atop of his body, pressing her big breasts into her chest, and proceeded to make love to him while he remained motionless! She rotated her pelvis vigorously, making the bed bounced furiously! She continued her love making until Bill began to reach a climax, and then he groaned in an orgasm!. He fell back in sexual exhaustion, and Atty slowed to a stop!

They lay there in a lovers' embrace, lips upon lips, until there was a sudden noise at the door. Someone was trying to get in but the chair was holding them out!

Atty quickly arose and drew on her slicker while she threw the covers over Bill as well. While she went to the door and removed the chair, Bill fumbled about in bed and his hand unsuspectingly found her panties. He stuffed the feminine undergarment under his hospital gown.

A nurse entered the room who wanted to take blood samples. Eyeing the lovely Atty she smiled knowingly as to why the door was braced shut. After the nurse left, Atty came back to the bed searching for her panties.

"I have them!" Bill asserted, "and I plan to keep them as a remembrance!"

"Why you naughty boy!" Atty responded with a laugh. Then she gave Bill a long passionate hug and kiss.

"I love you!" Atty said with tears now in her eyes! Then she stood up and suddenly left the room without a further word before Bill could tell her that he loved her as well.

Bill was shaken by her sudden departure. He loved her, and he realized that he probably would never see her again. His hand searched out her panties, and he felt them tenderly as if they were his lost love.

Indeed, the panties were a token of Bill's love affair with Atty, and he felt that besides memories it was the only thing he had of hers.

9

Bill was released from the hospital a few days later on Sunday, December 21st. While his wounds were fairly well healed, he was still stiff from lying in bed so long. In a few days he would be back up to his normal strength.

Bill had to report to fleet headquarters that he was officially discharged from the hospital, and then he was officially reassigned as commander of the *Pope*. Technically, until then Henry was officially in charge of the ship.

Afterwards, he went with Henry down to the small boat yard where the *Pope* was berthed to see about the repairs. Henry showed him around the ship and all the repair work in progress. Indeed, it was almost complete and the ship should be ready for duty in a couple of days.

Bill went up to the bridge where he was standing when the bomb struck, wounding him and others, and killing the ensign and the helmsman. The holes made by the flying shrapnel were all plugged and painted so that there was no sign of the violence that took place there almost two weeks ago. Then Bill went down to his own quarters and saw that everything seemed to be order, and that his personal belongs were not disturbed.

Afterward, Bill drove over to the Dutch Embassy in Manila. There was a big sign about its closure, but some Filipino maintenance men were still clearing up after the diplomats left. There was even a Dutchman or two wandering around supervising the final cleaning and closure of the facility. Bill was able to confirm with them that the Vanderpan family, including Atty, had flown out the previous Friday night. They flew to Batavia in the Dutch East Indies, the same as most of the Dutch personnel. Some of the diplomats actually went on to Australia.

Bill then drove over to Atty's house. It was all locked up with only a watchman looking after it, since it still belonged to the Netherlands government. Bill lingered in front of the house, remembering the wonderful time he had there with Atty.

And, of course, he vividly pictured his love affair with her. It had been such a glorious affair and his mind focused on the image of her beautiful naked female body, and he mentally went through the details of making love. And then there was the dinner and wine, and the sharing of their lives together. Finally, they had gone to sleep in each other's arms, like a loving couple.

Then Bill's mind turned pessimistic. He realized that he probably would never see her again. How tragic that was. At the moment all he had left of her were her panties, which he kept concealed on his person, which he touched lovingly.

Finally Bill returned to the *Pope*. He watched some of the repair work that Henry was directing, and then stayed on the bridge, planning for the refurbishment of the supplies for the ship.

The next morning, Monday the 22th, Bill heard the tragic news that a very large force of the Japanese army, complete with artillery and tanks, had landed at Lingayen Gulf, only some one hundred twenty miles north of Manila. A full-scale invasion of the Philippines was now taking place!

And there also were simultaneous landings of the Japanese on Mindanao and the capture of Davao way down on the most southern portion of the Philippines. This would help the Japanese to seal off escape from the Philippines and also to give them an advance base for attacking the Dutch East Indies which they probably intended to do.

The repair work on the *Pope* was finally completed the next afternoon, and all the missing crew had been replaced. Bill and the crew took the ship out of the small boat yard, and gave it a test run in the Manila Bay. He judged it to be fit for duty and proceeded to provision it for action.

The next day, Wednesday, December 24th, Manila was declared an "Open City", and all military personnel were relocated to Corregidor Island out at the entrance to Manila Bay. It was laced with tunnels to protect the defenders safe from air attack and the small island was heavily fortified.

Bill docked the *Pope* at the wharf of Corregidor to report to the Fleet Command that his ship was prepared for action. Actually, it now was the only surface warship left in the Philippines. Temporarily, Bill was directed to patrol the waters outside of Manila Bay, particularly for enemy submarines.

Bill was informed that Admiral Hart, the commander of the Asiatic Fleet, was shifting the Asiatic Fleet Command headquarters to Surabaya on Java in the Dutch East Indies shortly. Bill would be sent there as well.

Bill was quite elated when he heard this. Surabaya was on the same island, Java, as Batavia. He would be only some five hundred miles away from his love. It was a formidable distance but certainly one that he possibly could overcome.

Meanwhile, Bill learned that the Japanese army in north Luzon were pushing south towards Manila and were now only about eighty miles away. The outnumbered combined American-Filipino army units under General MacArthur were providing a determined defense but were being slowly driven back. Subic Bay Naval Station, meanwhile, was shut down, and all its facilities were destroyed.

At the same time more Japanese troops had landed in southern Luzon and were driving northward toward Manila. It appeared that Manila would fall to the Japanese soon. Bill was certainly glad that Atty had already left when she did.

Then, despite the declaration that Manila was an Open City, Japanese planes bombed it for the first time. The end was near!

Bill spent the next day, Christmas, patrolling outside Manila Bay, but at night he was allowed back in so he and his crew would celebrate the Holiday. On the following day, he was summoned to Corregidor Island again for a meeting with the remaining Navy command.

Bill was directed to leave Manila Bay that night and proceed at all speed to Surabaya to join the rest of the fleet. He was warned, however, that the Japanese had just occupied the major naval facility at Jolo in the Sula Archipelago, the most southern part of the Philippines.

All Filipino waters were now dangerous as Japanese ships could be prowling in all the seas around the Philippines. Bill was instructed to avoid daylight travel if at all possible.

Bill was walking out of the Corregidor tunnel to his ship just after noon when suddenly without warning enemy aircraft was spotted arriving overhead. Henry, as the ship's second in command, was under orders to clear the wharf when and if attacked.

Bill ran to the wharf as fast as he could while bombs were already falling. He just made it abroad as the *Pope* was casting off. By the time he reached the bridge, the ship was well on its way out into Manila Bay.

The *Pope* was obviously a good target for the bombers since it was the only surface warship around, and the planes made every effort to bomb it. They were flying too high for the ship's guns to retaliate, so Bill used every evasive maneuver to avoid the bombs.

As the planes took turns dropping their bombs Bill had to turn abruptly one way or another , or slow to stop, or back up, or race full speed ahead. This was an arduous task and continued for some two hours. Most of the bombs fell harmlessly some distance away. A few bombs, however, fell close enough to throw water up on the deck of the ship.

But the *Pope* suffered no damage or casualties. Finally the enemy planes departed, leaving the ship in peace.

Bill then docked the ship to top up his fuel and insure that it was fully supplied and equipped.

This gave him and the crew had a chance to rest before sunset and their departure that evening. It also gave Bill a chance to carefully study the charts of the seas they would be sailing and plan the precise route they should take. Then he advised his officers his course of action.

And finally they had a good meal before saying goodbye to Manila. Bill had been in this area for well over a month now, and he was glad he was heading southward toward his love.

10

As ordered, Bill sailed the *Pope* out of Manila Bay shortly after it was fully dark on December 27th. He ran without any navigation lights as he passed through the South Channel and out into the South China Sea in case any Japanese vessels should happened to be waiting for him. He kept the crew at general quarters during this time. Fortunately, they did not encounter any enemy ships.

Nevertheless, as Bill turned south he purposefully kept close to the coast to avoid detection. Then when the Pope passed through the Verde Island Passage into the interior seas of the Philippines he allowed the crew to relax to some extent. It was highly unlikely that any Japan ships would venture into these waters where they could so easily be detected and trapped.

The Pope sailed southward down passed Mindoro Island and eventually reached Panay Island. When Bill passed Panay he turned the ship through the narrow channel between Panay and Negros Islands. He was sure that Japanese ships would not penetrate into this area, but nevertheless he kept the crew on alert anyway, although in a more relaxed mode. Again, the *Pope* did not come across any enemy ships during its trip south.

It was early morning just before sunrise when the *Pope* headed for concealment on Negros Island. From his study of the charts Bill had selected an ideal spot for them to spend the next day.

He nosed the ship into the remote Campomanes Bay on the western side of Negros Island. Because of its deep water,

Bill was able to dock the ship close to and parallel with the beach. Then he had the crew secure lines to trees fore and aft to draw the ship in as close as possible. Then the crew collected palm fronds to cover the ship as much as possible to hopefully conceal it from Japanese aircraft searching for American targets.

The crew now had an opportunity to relax all day long while hoping not to be detected. Indeed, they able to sleep most of the day except when alerted that enemy air planes were approaching. Then they might have to make a quick exit if required. Indeed, several times enemy planes flew directly overhead, but the ship was not spotted. Apparently, the camouflaged ship blended into the surrounding trees along the shoreline.

Bill had originally planned that after leaving the Philippines he would continue southward via the Makassar Strait between the eastern coast of Borneo and the western coast of Celebes, as being the shortest way to Surabaya on Java in the Dutch East Indies. But listening to radio reports during the day, he was alerted to the fact the Japanese warships had been sighted patrolling around the northern part of Borneo. Since this would put the ship in possible danger Bill decided to take the much longer route around the eastern coast of Celebes.

In either case he would have to sail through the Sulu Sea in the southern Philippines in which Japanese ships might be patrolling. He would travel at night and as close as possible to the eastern side of the Sea hopefully to avoid detection. The most dangerous part would be passing through the small inlands of the Sulu Archipelago where he knew that the

Japanese had just recently captured the major naval station of Jolo. By now the station would be a harbor for Japanese warships.

As soon as it was dark, the *Pope* pushed off again southward into the Sulu Sea. Bill felt that their chances of encountering Japanese ships at night were minimal but the crew was kept on full alert. The Sulu Archipelago with the major naval base at Jolo, however, was a different matter. The Japanese probably might have a big concentration of Japanese ships in that area.

Accordingly, as Bill approached the Sulu Archipelago near midnight he turned off his running lights, and passed through the islands just some thirty miles north of Jolo without any incident. The *Pope* entered into the Celebes Sea and continued southward away from the Philippines towards Manado on the northeastern tip of the Celebes Island.

By morning the ship was well out of waters of the Philippines and heading toward the Dutch East Indies. Everyone was quite pleased to be out of harm's way and they could fully relax.

But suddenly shortly after eight o'clock in the morning a four-engine Japanese seaplane was sighted some eight miles out and heading in their direction. Battle stations were again sounded. Since the plane kept out of the range of their guns, Bill would have to rely on taking evasive actions instead. But when the plane made a bombing run, it turned away at the last moment and did not release any bombs. It did this a number of times without dropping any bombs. It was a very unnerving process for the whole crew.

The situation got worse about ten o'clock when another four-engine Japanese seaplane joined the first one. Then the two planes took turns making bombing runs, but always turning away at the last moment. Needless to say, this continuous threat kept everyone on the ship quite nervous. Any of the runs might be for real, and the planes might actually release their bombs.

This went for hour after hour. Since the Japanese now knew where his ship was located, Bill tried to radio an Allied station to provide them with his position and the actions of the Japanese planes to the Allies, but he was unable to make any contact.

Then with great relief, about two o'clock in the afternoon two Allied PBY seaplanes were sighted coming from the south. The *Pope* tried to exchange light signals with the planes but they failed. They remained about an hour and then flew off to the south.

It was then that the Japanese seaplanes finally began to actually attack the *Pope*. The first plane made an actual bombing and machine gun run at about 5,000 feet elevation. The ship's guns were now able to fire at the plane, while Bill was able to successively take evasive action to evade the bombs. When the second plane made its run at an even lower elevation the ship's guns apparently were able to drive it away.

Then two Japanese twin-engine torpedo planes joined in the attack. They circled out of range while the two seaplanes made two more bombing runs each. Bill managed to use every evasion trick necessary to avoid the bombs. Some of them, however, dropped fairly close but did not do any damage.

Then the torpedo planes attacked. The first came in just fifty feet over the water and the ships guns apparently had some success. Nevertheless, at some five hundred yards out it discharged two torpedoes that caused Bill to twist the ship to avoid them. Meanwhile, the second torpedoes plane came in from a different direction and launched two more torpedoes. Bill had to swing about and come to a complete stop to make them miss the ship by just two feet.

With the *Pope* dead in the water, one of the seaplanes made another run, and Bill had to surge full throttle to avoid its bombs.

Finally, having dropped sixteen bombs and four torpedoes the Japanese planes flew off to the joy of everyone on the ship.

The attack had lasted most of day and it had been quite an ordeal for the crew. But due to clever evasive maneuvering, the ship was not damaged and the morale of the crew was high.

It was now almost six o'clock in the evening, with night rapidly approaching, and the *Pope* was finally able to continue its journey southward. They were at the northern tip of Celebes near the city of Manado, and Bill tired again to radio the Allied stations again but again without success.

Shortly afterwards as dusk was descending three twin-engine bombers were sighted, and the exhausted crew were brought to battle stations again. Soon, however, the planes were recognized as Australian. The *Pope* flashed the Anglo-Dutch-US recognition signal, and it seemed as if the planes responded positively.

But then one of the planes made bombing run at the ship, and Bill swung sharply to starboard to avoid the bomb. This sudden motion caused one seaman to be cast overboard. Two more bombing and machine gun runs were made, and while all bombs missed, one exploded nearby sending shrapnel into the ship. One seaman was killed and three men were wounded, while the steam line to the steering engine was ruptured.

While darkness caused the bombers to leave, the *Pope* was in bad shape. The starboard engine was overheating and the ship had to proceed only on its port engine. Both fuel and feed water were in short supply.

Bill crossed into the Molucca Sea and headed eastward to the small island of Maitara near Ternate Island in the Maluku Group where they were able to conceal the ship again. They reached Maitara Island at dawn, December 29th.

They found an ideal harbor to the hide the *Pope* while they made temporary repair. As before the crew used palm fronds to camouflage the ship, just in case. Bill again sent out a report as to the whereabouts of his ship, the plane attacks, and the condition of his ship. This time his report was acknowledged. Hopefully Allied planes would not attack the *Pope* again. The crew could now relax without fear of being attacked – by friend or foe.

Bill used the ship's motor launch to visit the Dutch military commander at the nearby little town of Ternate in order to get some supplies. He was able to obtain a good supply of portable water, bread, and fresh fruits, but no fuel was available. Instead, however, Bill figured they had enough fuel to reach the Dutch base at Ambon, some three hundred miles to the south.

Meanwhile, Henry worked that day and the next day to make some temporary repairs, sufficiently to make the ship seaworthy again. Finally at sunset on the second day they cast off again. But soon it became apparent that the starboard was not going to work. Instead, they had to rely on just the port engine to limp along on their way south.

They arrived in Ambon without any further incidents early in the afternoon of December 31st. Now the crew of the *Pope*, including Bill, had a good chance to rest for a couple days.

11

While laying over in Ambon, the starboard engine was again being repaired in a make-shift manner. The facilities there were fairly crude so they would have to wait until they reached in Surabaya for a better fix.

While Henry was supervising the repair of the *Pope*, Bill visited the military commander to find out why his ship was attacked by Allied planes. He was told that Manado, a town on Celebes Island that he had passed had been heavily bombed a few days earlier, and they were afraid that a landing party would soon follow. When the American PBY pilots saw the *Pope* heading toward Manado, and being "convoyed" by Japanese bombers, they mistook the ship to be a Japanese light cruiser. The Australian bombers were thereby sent out to sink the supposed enemy.

Also, Bill learned that Ambon was at the center of the legendary "spice islands". These were what the early Portuguese ships were looking for, although they eventually passed into Dutch hands. These spices were highly valued in Europe and greatly spurred the European commercial interests thrust into Asia.

Meanwhile, it being New Year's Eve the crew was given the opportunity to go ashore in groups and enjoy some liquid refreshments. As the day passed into the evening, the Dutch military celebrated with a party. Half the ship's crew was allowed to enjoy themselves at an early session headed by Henry, and the other half headed by Bill at a later session. But by the time the later session started, however, most of the men were too tired and preferred to get a good night's sleep instead.

It was late in the evening by the time Bill himself went to the officer's club to celebrate New Year's Eve. Only a few officers joined him, Ensign Roberts among them. It was mainly a Dutch crowd in the club with a few Australians. All were male with a few local Indonesian girlfriends providing some feminine charm. Generally, all the men were military, with a scattering of some civilian government people as well.

Bill was setting at the bar in the room when suddenly he was surprised to see Mr. Vanderpan, Atty's father! He was just walking out of the club with a couple of friends. Bill immediately jumped up to intercept him before he left.

"Mr. Vanderpan …." Bill called out as he stretched out my hand.

As Atty's father turned, however, Bill was quite surprised to see his face frown as if he was not pleased to see him! And he did not replicate to Bill's outstretched hand. Bill was quite puzzled by the man's unfriendliness. .

"Does Atty happen to be with you, sir?" Bill continued hopefully in a puzzled voice.

"Commander," Mr. Vanderpan replied sternly, "I do not want you to see my daughter anymore!"

Bill was quite shocked by the content and tone of what he was saying.

"My daughter is engaged to be married to a close family friend of ours!" Mr. Vanderpan continued! "And we do not want you interfering in their marriage in any way!"

Bill was shocked speechless!

"Do understand me, Commander? You are not to see my daughter again!" Without waiting for Bill's reply, Atty's father turned and walked out with his friends.

Bill stood there dumbfounded, unable to move! Ensign Roberts, who knew about his affair with Atty, was standing right behind Bill and heard what had happened.

"What a horrible man!" Roberts exclaimed, as if to assure Bill of his support.

Bill just stood there looking at the door where Mr. Vanderpan had left. He was hardly able to absorb what the man had said to him.

Atty engaged to be married? Bill could not believe it! How could she be? She was so loving to him!

Finally, Bill recovered sufficiently to move back to the bar. Roberts followed him, still complaining about Atty's father! Bill did not pay attention to Roberts as he was still somewhat in a shock. Then he sat down on the bar stool and ordered a double whiskey!

Bill sat at the bar slowly drinking his whiskey! Roberts kept on chatting, but Bill was not listening as he was absorbed in his own thoughts. He kept on thinking about Atty and how beautiful and loving she was! How could it all be so wrong?

Bill was about to order another double whisky when a he was touched lightly on his shoulder!

"Hello, Admiral Daring!" came the soft and sweet female voice!

Startled out of his misery, he swung around and there was Atty standing right next to him. He should have realized that she had entered the room for suddenly it was silent, and now everyone was staring at her – the beautiful, blue eyed, blonde woman!

Bill was stunned by the sight of her, but she leaned forward, flung her arms around his neck, and kissed him on his lips!

"But …. But …." Bill stammered when he was free! "You are engaged!"

"Oh, yes," Atty added nonchalantly! "But I don't love him! I love you!"

"But …. But how come are you going to marry him?"

"Well, let me explain." Atty tried to calm Bill. She sat down next to him at the bar. Roberts moved away and chased away the crowd of men that had gathered around them.

Atty related how she had run away with first no good husband, the father of her young son still in Holland, whom she had married against her parent's objections. They had warned her that her boyfriend was no good but she was young and would not listen.

Now she was older and wiser. She wanted to marry a safe and sane man. This time she was going to follow her parents' advice.

She had known Hans all her life, and both their families were very close. They all had assumed that Atty and Hans would eventually get married. This was quite common in Europe. Indeed, she liked him even though she did not really love him.

Indeed, they had even been engaged when she ran away with another man, her first husband. She had hurt Hans badly. Now she wanted to make up it to him – and to her parents!

Bill tried to explain how useless this was. She was sacrificing her life just to please her parents and a man whom she had wronged. She would be sorry the rest of her life. Bill tried to convince her in the most serious way. But she interrupted his dialog in a most light-hearted way.

"Come on," Atty exclaimed excitedly, "it's almost midnight! Come dance with me!"

Bill could not resist her, and he followed her to the dance floor where only a few men were dancing with some local Indonesian girls. Bill tried to bring up the subject of Atty's engagement again.

"Tut, tut!" Atty objected, "not now! It's New Year's Eve!"

As Bill held Atty in his arms, he completely surrendered to the feel of her female body against his and the smell of her perfume. His arguments against her marrying some other man seem to just disappear as they danced together. At least he had her now – tonight. And no one knows what would happen tomorrow in this crazy world at war!

Then came the New Year's Eve count down and …"Happy New Year!"

Atty embraced Bill tightly and they kissed each other passionately!

"Happy New Year, Admiral Darling!" she exclaimed.

"Happy New Year, my crazy Dutch girl!" Bill responded, laughingly.

Then they danced again while kissing.

Finally, the people started leaving, and Atty grabbed Bill's hand as she led him away.

"Come with me!" Atty invited him with a twinkle in her eye.

Bill did not resist, and Atty led him to the government car she was using that was parked in a remote darkened area. Rather than opening the front door as would be normal, she opened the back door instead, and smiling mischievously she beckoned him in.

Knowingly, Bill climb into the back seat, and Atty climbed in after him -- and locked the car doors after her. Then they were in each other's arms and kissing passionately!

Bill's hand automatically searched out one of Atty's breasts and fondled them without encountering any resistance. Indeed, she leaned forward and unzipped the back of her dress, and Bill immediately unfastened her brassiere.

As Atty's naked breasts were exposed, Bill buried his face in them, and then started sucking on her big hard nipples. Atty, meanwhile, lifted up and pulled her dress off and discarded her bra. Then just as quickly she pulled down her panties, and she was now completely naked sitting in the back seat of the car!

Bill, on the other hand, pulled off his shirt and yanked his pants and shorts down to his ankles! Now they were both literally naked and were rolling around naked in the back seat together, male body to female body!

While Bill sat back in the seat, Atty slipped onto his lap! She carefully inserted his manhood into her body, and they proceeded to make love together. Bill felt like they were like teenagers back in the States indulging in sex in the back seat of a car! It was not long before both of them obtained a sexual fulfillment, and they lay motionless in each other's arms, continuing to kiss each other tenderly.

Finally they stirred, and clumsily got dressed. They climbed out of the back seat of the car, Atty then got into the driver's seat. She offered to give Bill a ride down to wharf.

"You're not really going to marry that man, are you?" Bill asked her seriously.

"Now not, silly," Atty responded. "Now it is just you and me."

"But, but …." Bill tried to argue.

"Kiss me, darling!" Atty insisted

Obediently Bill complied. He embraced her and passionately kissed her for a long time.

Atty then drove the car down to the wharf. Bill tried to bring up the subject again, but Atty just kept saying that it was unimportant. They kissed again and Bill finally got out of the car.

Atty called out to him merrily ….

"Come and see me in Batavia!" Then she was gone.

12

Bill woke up the next morning, New Year's Day, which normally was a holiday. But for him and the crew of the *Pope*, it was a normal work day preparing for their continuing trip onward to Surabaya.

While Henry was still attending to the temporary repairs, Bill caught a ride up the government house. He wanted to see Atty again before he left, but he was advised that she was already gone. She had flown out with her father earlier that morning.

Bill was still bothered by the fact that she was engaged to another man, even if she did not love him. He wasn't sure how he could get to Batavia, which was at the opposite end of Java from Surabaya, some five hundred miles apart. But he promised himself that he would get there somehow or die trying. Meanwhile, he still had her panties, which he treasured more than anything else.

By late afternoon, Henry had made all the necessary repairs that he could make with the limited resources at hand. After fueling and adding a few more supplies, the *Pope* was ready to disembark.

They cast off and sailed through the Banda Sea most of that night, and after passing the south side of Celebes Island early in the morning they entered the Java Sea. They finally reached Surabaya on the east end of Java late that afternoon.

Surabaya was located inland from the Java Sea in a well-protected strait between Java and its large neighboring island of Madura. As they entered the port Bill could see how well it was protected. He also noticed how pretty the city of Surabaya was.

Bill needed to get final repairs for the *Pope*, and he was directed to a repair wharf. After docking he and his crew were taken over to the destroyer wharves to be with the rest of the men from Destroyer Division 59.

The other three destroyers were there, birthed in a camouflaged setting to avoid detection from the air. The wharves were located at a remote end of the naval base. Bill was informed that the other two destroyer divisions were out on convoy duty. The three divisions took turns, two out of convoy duty and the third resting in Surabaya.

Bill, of course, had to report to Fleet Headquarters, now stationed in Surabaya. He related his harrowing experiences coming down from the Philippines and being attacked by both Japanese and Allied planes. He mentioned about the Japanese occupation of the southern Philippines and the shelling of Manado, on Celebes Island, in the Dutch East Indies.

It was obvious that in due course the Japanese would probably be coming into the Dutch East Indies soon as well, particularly since that is where the oil was located. Japan desperately needed oil to fuel their vast military machine.

Bill heard the sad news that Japanese soldiers had marched into Manila the previous day. The remaining American and Filipino army units, meanwhile, were retreating to the Bataan

Peninsula and the Corregidor Island where they planned to be able to hold off the Japanese for a long while.

Surabaya was now the home port for all the American surface ships of the Asiatic Fleet, including the heavy cruiser *Houston* and the light cruisers *Marblehead* and *Boise*. In addition, the Fleet also included the thirteen "four-pipers" destroyers. Most of the ships, however, were out on convoy duty of one sort or another.

While resting in Surabaya, Phil the division commander and Bill's old friend, took Bill and Henry along on a short tour of Surabaya. They drove to the downtown area of the city and along the waterfront facing the large harbor. This latter contained ships and boats of all types, from modern oil tankers to many kinds of old-fashioned local sailing crafts. With the island of Madura across the straits as background, Surabaya was quite a picturesque town.

The naval officers had some refreshments at a local kafi, or café. Bill noticed that beer was brewed locally by Heineken, the famous Dutch brewery. As they sat there in an outdoor kafi on the waterfront away from the base but overlooking the civilian harbor, it seemed so peaceful. It certainly did not have a feeling that a war was being waged with Japan.

Then Phil took them for a short drive into the countryside where Bill saw field after field of rice paddies, something like he saw in the rural parts of the Philippines. People were working in the fields, and he noticed that some of them even had a flock of geese with them. Phil explained that he had been told that the geese feed on the insects that destroy the rice crop.

Then the officers headed back to the naval base.

13

Since the *Pope* would be laid up for a few days and the division not scheduled to go convoy duty until after that, Bill eagerly wanted to take up Atty's invitation to visit her in Batavia.

He had no phone contact, of course, and he just took a chance of going there anyway. On the next morning, January 3rd, he advised both Phil, his superior officer, and Henry where he was going and that he would be back the next morning. While Phil was not keen on letting him go, he did not disapprove the trip.

Since Batavia was the governmental center for the Dutch East Indies, and Surabaya was one its major naval base, Dutch naval planes shuttled back and forth routinely. Bill had checked on the flight schedules before he went to the airport.

Accordingly, Bill hopped a ride on a naval aircraft that was making a morning flight to Batavia. On the flight there, Bill sat next to a Dutch naval officer who could speak English and they chatted about the Japanese threat to the East Indies. It seemed inevitable that they would invade the Indies for the oil.

Atty had mentioned that she and her farther worked in the military government building in Kota, or the downtown center of the city. The Dutch officer promised to show Bill where it was since he was going there as well. When the plane landed, a government vehicle took them to Kota. When they arrived at the military building, they stood outside at the entrance gate to the court yard leading up to the building.

The officer knew Mr. Vanderpan, who was an important attaché, and of course his lovely daughter. Indeed, his eyes lit up with the mention of her. He was quite shocked when Bill mentioned that he was coming to see her. He then burst into a wondrous smile.

"What a lucky man you are!" the officer laughed.

Then he turned to talk in Dutch with the Indonesian guard at the outer gate to building. The officer turned back to Bill and told him that the father had already left, but that Miss Vanderpan should be coming out soon for lunch. Then the officer walked across the courtyard and into the building.

Bill waited patiently while looking across the open courtyard as people were slowly leaving the building. He wondered what her reaction would be when she saw him there waiting at the gate.

Suddenly, Bill spotted Atty coming out of the building. She looked as beautiful as ever. She was walking slowly across the courtyard as she and a male companion were talking earnestly in conversation. The man appeared a little shorter than Atty, who was tall for a girl, and stouter. Also, he appeared somewhat older.

Looking up, Atty then spotted Bill waiting for her and she burst into a big smile. She stopped and turned to the man with whom she was walking, and after a brief conversation he turned and walked back to the building. Atty watched him until he was in the building, then she turned and almost ran to the gate and threw herself into Bills arms.

“Hello, Admiral Darling,” she burst out, and then gave him a nice big kiss. After the greeting, Bill could not help but ask.

“Was that your fiancée?” he questioned, and Atty nodded affirmatively with a knowing smile.

“Yes, that is Hans,” she confirmed. “But I don’t love him,” she assured Bill, “he is only a good friend.”

“But why are you going to marry him?” Bill argued. But Atty just laughed and gave him another kiss.

“Don’t quibble!” She responded with another laugh.

Bill thought that it was strange to marry someone who was only a good friend. But then he was glad to have seen his “competition” and understood why she could not love him.

The Indonesian guard merrily greeted her, and then turned and blew his whistle to summon a cab.

“You can take me to lunch,” Atty laughed as they both climbed into the cab. “I know a very exotic place!”

Atty gave instructions in Indonesian to the driver, and then hugged Bill and gave him a peck on his cheek. Bill noticed that they drove along a wide canal, almost like they were in

Amsterdam, but like the Philippines the street was crowded with cars, carts, bicycles, animals, and people.

Atty explained to Bill that while the people in Central and East Java spoke Javanese, in West Java the people spoke Sundanese. But here in Batavia where the people come from all over the islands with hundreds of different languages, Bahasa Indonesia or the newly developed "national language", was usually spoken. Some of the more educated Indonesians could also speak Dutch.

They then turned along another canal into Menteng, the rich suburb of the city where most of the Dutch nationals lived. Finally they turned again and eventually stopped in front of a fancy restaurant.

"This is a real nice Dutch-Indonesian restaurant," Atty announced, "but expensive! But I am sure an American can afford it!"

She laughed and gave Bill a hug. As they entered the foyer of the restaurant a gong rang out, and Bill was surprised to see eight young pretty Indonesian girls dressed in Sundanese national dress greet them. They escorted the couple into the restaurant proper and seated them at a table overlooking a beautiful garden.

The head waitress approached and Atty spoke Indonesian with her. Soon drinks arrived at the table, Heineken beer for Bill and tea for Atty.

Then the Indonesian girls came out with the first serving. Atty explained that they were having Indonesian "Rijsttafel". It actually is a Dutch word that literally translates to "rice table". It is an elaborate meal adapted by the Dutch from Indonesia and consists of many side dishes served in small portions. It is accompanied by rice prepared in several different ways. Popular side dishes include egg rolls, sambals, satay, fish, fruit, vegetables, pickles, and nuts.

Atty warned Bill to eat just a little of each since the courses would keep coming and coming. Indeed, the eight pretty girls served one dish followed by another in an almost endless manner. Bill did not fully follow Atty's advice and he soon became quite stuffed.

Afterwards, they just relaxed with coffee, brandy, and a cigar for him and tea for her. They chatted a while before Bill brought up the subject of her fiancé again.

"Oh, please don't," Atty begged him. "Let's just enjoy our being together again, and don't worry about some future time."

Bill thought best not to continue, so he kissed Atty in agreement. He finally paid the bill, which was expensive, and then they were escorted out graciously by the pretty Indonesian girls.

Out on the street again, they did not use a regular taxi this time. Instead Atty summoned a bijak, a bicycle propelled "taxi" with a seat for two. She explained that it was the normal means of transportation in Batavia.

"Where are we going in this?" Bill asked wonderingly.

"To my house! It is nearby." Atty responded with a big smile and hug. "You don't mind seeing me home, do you?" she continued with a laugh. "I might even invite you in if you behave yourself."

Of course, Bill did not mind. Indeed, he would just love to spend the afternoon – and the night – with the beautiful lady!

Atty lived also in Menteng, and soon they reached her house. It was located amidst some very large and fancy mansions, but Atty's house was much smaller, although still a substantial building. Obviously it was meant for a single occupant or two, as normally the Dutch residents rotated in and out from Holland on a regular every other year basis.

They were greeted by the jaga, the building guard who stood on duty all night long. He smiled broadly at Bill and even gave the American naval officer a smart salute. Atty spoke to him sharply in Sundanese, and he nodded in agreement with a big smile as the pair passed into her house.

Inside were several female servants, a cook and two maids as Atty described them to Bill. They too smiled broadly at Bill and giggled among themselves. Again, Atty spoke to them sharply in Sundanese, and they all passed into the kitchen area still giggling.

Then she took Bill by his hand and led him into her bedroom, locking the door behind her.

"Now Admiral Darling, could you help me with my dress?" Atty asked as she nonchalantly turned her back to him.

Needless to say, Bill jumped to the task eagerly and dutifully unzipped the dress down her back. Atty pulled the garment off her shoulders and let the dress fall to the floor. Stepping out of it, Atty turned around clad only in her brassiere and panties, and posed her gorgeous body for Bill's inspection.

"Do you see anything you like?" she asked provocatively with a mischievous smile on her face.

"Yes, everything!" Bill responded eagerly as he grabbed her lustfully in his arms and kissed her passionately!

Even while he was kissing her, Bill was fumbled with her bra strap, finally managing to unfasten it! Atty shrugged her shoulders and let the garment fall free and letting her breasts flop into sight. But before Bill could grasp them, however, she backed off and fell backwards onto the bed! Clad only in her panties, she provocatively raised her arms above her head, thrusting her breasts upwards, and letting them bobble about on her chest.

"Now don't you dare steal my panties!" Atty declared with a giggle! "You've already stolen one pair of them!"

Bill, of course, immediately grabbed her panties and pulled them off her, while Atty did not resist at all. Now fully naked she made no effort to cover her breasts or her pelvis with her hands, and instead spread her legs wide apart so Bill could see "all her female attributes".

"Remember, Admiral Darling, you are an officer and a gentleman!" Atty teased him as Bill quickly pulled off his own clothes and jumped on the bed with her. She laughed playfully as the two of them rolled around naked together on the bed!

Bill caressed her Atty's naked female body, squeezed her big breasts, and sucked on her nipples until she was groaning! He finally positioned himself on top of her, and kneeling between her legs he entered her womanhood!

Then they made love! Bill did it nice and slowly to prolong the sexual pleasure as long as possible and hopefully make Atty come to a climax as well! He could not hold back long and soon he was making love to her vigorously and she responded in kind! Finally both of them enjoyed sexual satisfaction!

Bill slid off the top of Atty's body and cuddled her closely. They lay there together in sexual fulfillment for a long time.

Suddenly, however, voices came from the other room, those of the female servants and that of a man!

"It's Hans!" Atty exclaimed in a panic! "Hurry into the bathroom!"

Bill jumped up, grabbed his pants and shirt and made for the bathroom! Atty followed with his shoes and socks! Then as Bill returned for his shorts, Atty was covering herself in a dressing gown! As she prepared to unlock the bedroom door, Bill locked himself in the bathroom.

He heard voices, including Atty's, from the other room as he was dressing. It was all in Dutch and it seemed almost as if they were arguing. Then suddenly he was in a panic as he remembered that he had left his naval officer hat in the living room! He cursed himself – what a dumb thing to do!

Then Bill heard a loud male voice, and he was afraid that Hans may have discovered it! But there was nothing he could do about it now, other than just wait.

Bill had to wait some time before the voices became lower and then stopped all together. Finally, Atty came to the bathroom door. When Bill unlocked it she was standing there with a guilty look on her face as she held his hat in her hand.

"He found this!" Atty exclaimed, and then burst out laughing. "I explained that it was left over from one of father's meetings here. Hans doesn't work for the navy, and he can't really tell the difference between Dutch, British, or American caps."

"Should I go?" Bill asked.

"No," Atty responded. "He is on his way to the Governors Palace in Bogor, and he will stay there overnight" she explained. "So you can stay here with me tonight! You don't mind, do you?" With this she placed his hat on her head and kissed him.

"Of course not!" Bill replied quite truthfully!

Atty walked back into the bedroom, turned facing Bill and casually removed her dressing gown, displaying her naked female body to him. Then she lay back in bed again.

"Are you going to join me?"

Bill did not need a second invitation. He quickly discarded all his clothes again and lay down on the bed with Atty and gathered her in his arms. They lay together chatting and dozing for most of the rest of the afternoon. Then they made love again, almost like newlyweds.

As evening came around Atty got up, dressed in her gown again, and went out to arrange a little supper with the servants in the kitchen. Bill though that it was appropriate that he wear all his clothes, leaving nothing behind, and keep his cap close at hand.

Then they had a candlelight dinner, with assorted sandwiches and spreads, and wine. This followed by a little coffee and brandy for Bill and tea for Atty. They talked a lot -- about their past – and avoided the future.

Bill related his experiences with boats when he was quite young. He himself had a little sailboat, and one time he took two of his friends out through the Golden Gate Strait into the Pacific Ocean. When they tried to return, however, the tide was flowing out, which was very strong at the strait, and they hardly made any headway at all.

Indeed, large waves were rolling in from the Pacific Ocean that swelled quite high through the strait. Bill was sitting on the stern and looking up at the incoming swell. They seem to be towering over the little boat, and he was worried that the waves might just roll right over them. But instead the stern of the boat rode the waves beautifully, up and down, up and down, up and down. While it was scary, this experience made him trust the seaworthiness of boats.

"I don't want to know about your silly boats," Atty insisted, "I want to know about your girlfriends."

"I told you that I didn't have any steady girlfriends." Bill replied.

"All right then," Atty retorted, "what was the name of the girl you first kissed?"

Bill had to think for a moment. "I guess it was Helen," he confessed.

"Who was the girl to whom you first made love?" She continued without hesitation.

"Now wait a minute!" Bill retorted! "Aren't you getting a little personal?"

"Well, not really," Atty replied defensively. "Why don't you ask me?"

"All right then, "he replied, 'who did you sleep with first!"

"None of your business!" Atty snapped, and then she had a big laugh.

They carried on like this for a while and then they retired early. They cuddled naked in bed talking, joking, and laughing. Finally, they made love again. Bill made sure that Atty received as much pleasure out of it and as he did before he finished. When they both were fulfilled they cuddled in each other's arms and fell asleep.

They got up early in the morning, and after a quick breakfast they took a taxi to Atty's office. Then the taxi took Bill to the airport. He caught another navy shuttle plane back to Surabaya – thinking about Atty all the way.

14

When Bill arrived back in Surabaya he instead had to start thinking of his ship, the *Pope*. He immediately went down to the yard, and found that it was all repaired. Henry felt that the ship was fully seaworthy even though it was not in perfect condition. The crew was quickly assembled and the ship was taken over to destroyer wharves.

The three other destroyers were waiting there. The destroyer squadrons had been reorganized somewhat since coming to Surabaya. Commander Phil Tower's Division included the *John D. Ford* as his flagship as before, which was commanded by Bill's friend Al Hawkins. The *Pope*, commanded by Bill, was now back in the Division, again as before. Newly added were the *Parrott*, commanded by Keith Jones, and the *Paul Jones*, commanded by Richard Rogers, his other old friend from the Atlantic Fleet days.

"Well, how is the beautiful girl friend?" Al asked, and the others all laughed. By now most of the officers in the Division knew that Bill was carrying on with a Dutch girlfriend, and some had actually met her at the Thanksgiving dinner at Subic Bay Station. Those who had seen her vowed for her beauty, and actually they all were quite envious of Bill.

But now it was Phil's Division's turn for convey duty. Phil explained the operation to the four skippers, which entailed escorting some oil tankers out of Tarakan and Balikpapan on Borneo as they were expected to be attacked by the Japanese soon. While there were no Japanese surface warships in the waters of the Dutch East Indies, there was always the danger of Japanese submarines lurking about to attack the Allied supply lines

Late in the morning of January 4th, the same day that Bill had returned from Batavia, the four destroyers steamed out of Surabaya. Phil and Al headed the group in the *John D. Ford*, followed by Bill in the *Pope*, Keith in the *Parrott*, and Dick in the *Paul Jones.* They crossed the Java Sea and entered the Makassar Strait between Borneo and the Celebes.

They arrived at Tarakan, the most northerly port on Borneo, the next afternoon. The Dutch engineers were getting ready to sabotage the existing oil wells in case of a Japanese attack. Meanwhile, all the resident tankers were filled with oil, and the destroyers escorted them southward!

They reached Balikpapan the following morning. This was a major Dutch oil depot which they hoped to retain as it was rich with oil deposits. If the Japanese attacked the East Indies for oil, which was expected, this city would certainly be their prime target. Again, Dutch engineers were preparing explosives to take the oil wells out of service if necessary. They also prepared to destroy as much as possible in case the Japanese came.

All the filled tankers joined the convoy as it headed back to the Java Sea. Once the convoy reached the Java Sea, the oil tankers spit up. Some of them turned eastward to Tanjung-Priok, the port of Batavia. Some headed to Surabaya, and others were going to Tjilatjap on the southern or Indian Ocean side of Java.

The four destroyers accompanied the tankers going to Surabaya and returned tom port.

15

Since Bill's Division now had a few days off, Bill took the opportunity to make another trip to Batavia to see Atty. They had previously arranged a telephone system because Bill had to use the phone in the Task Force or the Destroyer Squadron headquarters. While Atty had a phone in her house, he probably would have to contact her during the day at the government center. In order to disguise themselves somewhat, Bill was known as "Doctor" Taylor and Atty as "Nurse Vanderpan.

When Bill arrived back in Surabaya he called Atty at her home and told her he would be coming up in the morning. She said that she would pick him up at the airport with a car and driver and that he should plan to be gone for at least two nights. She wanted to take him to someplace special up in the mountains, which could be cool at night. She warned him to bring a jacket.

So in the next morning, January 7th, Bill caught the Dutch naval shuttle plane over to Batavia again. As promised, Atty was there with a car to meet him, but discreetly she waited in the background until the other people had left. Then she greeted him with a hug and kiss.

The two of them sat in the back seat as the driver headed out of Batavia and drove some thirty miles into the interior to Bogor. They slowly gained altitude as they approached the city since it was backed up to some mountains in the interior of Java. Because of this, Atty explained, it rains in Bogor almost every late afternoon. This cools the temperature somewhat and makes it much more pleasant that the hot and humid Batavia.

For this reason, the Dutch built a Governor's Palace in Bogor to allow the governor to escape the heat and turmoil of the capital whenever he felt liked it. The grounds of the palace are very extensive, and one of the previous governors started collecting plants from all over the world. It now has a large biological garden for which the Dutch were quite proud.

From Bogor the road started climbing more steeply as it passed though village after village crowded next to the road. In the process, they passed from rice fields to large tea plantations. Owned and operated by the Dutch government, Bill could see the Indonesians working in the tea bushes. Atty explained that all the people in this part of Java, outside of Batavia itself, were Sundanese who were quite different from the Javanese farther east.

Then they climbed above the tea plantations and into coniferous forests. Finally they reached Puncak Pass, some 6,000 feet above sea level. The temperature was now much cooler than below. Atty had arranged that they would stay there in the Puncak Pass Lodge for two nights as Mr. and Mrs. Veldman! It was a pretty little lodge, and from the dining room where they took a late lunch it had a wonderful view eastward over the lands below.

Atty explained that Puncak Pass was on the main road to Bandung, the large city in the interior to which the Dutch were planning to move the capital from Batavia. Because Dutch travelers often stopped at the Lodge for lunch, Atty purposely picked a remote spot in the restaurant, but one where she had a good view of the front entrance door. Besides, it was largely past the normal lunch time, and the customers were very few now.

They had a wonderful lunch of nasi goring, or fried rice, with an egg on top and with some shrimp crackers. And then finally they were escorted down the steps on the east side of the Lodge to a small cabin. It was quite comfortable and had a fireplace with a lot of wood stored next to it. Atty warned that it could get quite cold at night.

Soon after they settled in they hugged and kissed. Then Bill lit a fire and both stripped off their clothes and wrapped themselves with blankets in front of the fireplace. Bill pulled up a nice big and soft chair for Atty and he sat on a pillow on the floor in front of her. As they chatted she opened her blanket and pulled Bill's head against her naked body! He kissed her intimately! And she just sat back in the big soft chair and enjoyed it!

Atty collapsed back in the chair in sexual fulfillment. Bill pulled the blanket around her to keep her warm and laid his head on her abdomen. While they lay for a long time Bill reached his hands up her body and grasped her breasts, slowly massaging them.

After a while Atty reached down and pulled Bill's head up to her breasts, letting him suck on her nipples! She then raised her arms up behind her head to make her breasts stick out very prominently as sucked one nipple and then the other!

Bill knelt on the floor in front of the chair, leaned forward and sucked each nipple in turn. When Atty was all "worked up",

Bill rose up and inserted his male sexual organ into to her female body! Then he made love to her, slowly at first while at the same time leaning forward to suck her breast nipples again, one after the other! Bill sped up his motions, and it wasn't long before he had a nice orgasm!

They remained in the chair, with Bill's head now in Atty's lap for a while. Before they went to sleep, however, they shifted to the bed and crawled under the covers. Then wrapped in each other's arms and went to sleep.

They woke up later in the afternoon, and Bill built up the fire again. Atty spread out some thick blankets in front of the fireplace and they made love again in the normal way right on the floor in front of the fire!

Then they finally got dressed.

When they went outside it was dark, and they had to wear jackets as the air was now chilly. They walked up the steps to the dining room of the Lodge. Atty carefully looked over the room to insure no one she knew was there, and then they sat down for a nice dinner.

After a few drinks, they had a formal dinner together in the candlelight and with wine. After dinner Bill had coffee and brandy while Atty had tea. It was all so romantic, and they really enjoyed it.

It was just like a honeymoon, Atty giggled. Indeed, they chit-chatted, held hands, and even kissed a bit – just like a honeymoon couple!

Bill was tempted to bring up the subject of her fiancé. But he did not to break the loving mood, so he dropped the idea.

Later on the two of them went back down the steps to their cabin again. It was quite cold now. Bill built a big fire and Atty pushed the big soft chair in front of fireplace. She wanted to make love again like they had before.

Atty undressed and sat back in the chair wrapped in a blanket, and raised her arms above her head to thrust her breasts forward! Bill knelt on the floor in front of her, sucked each of her nipples, and lowered his head to her pelvis and kissed her *mons veneris*!

Atty loved the stimulation, and soon Bill adjusted his position to insert his manhood into her body! Then he proceeded to make love to her! He continued until they had a nice orgasm!

After making love, they hopped into bed and went to sleep for the night in each other's arms. Indeed, it had been like a honeymoon! They had made love three times that day – just like honeymooners!

The next morning Atty dashed to the bathroom, which had an electric heater, and drew a bath with lots of bubbles. She jumped into it and called on Bill to come and bathe her! He came, but instead he jumped into the tub with her. Then laughingly they bathed each other. And needless to say, they played with each other in the process!

When they got dressed they walked up the steps to the Lodge again. After Atty quickly surveyed the dining to make sure no was there who would recognize her, they sat down for a nice leisurely breakfast. The sun was out and they had a beautiful view to the east out across Java.

After breakfast, Bill and Atty walked across the road and into the woods on western side of the lodge. Then they began to hike up the slope of Mount Pangrango. The summit, almost 10,000 feet elevation, was only some seven miles away but they had no intention of climbing that far.

Instead, after they were quite alone in the woods, mischievously Atty wanted to go *au naturel* in the remote wilderness! Bill certainly approved of the idea, and finding a thick thicket, they laughingly stripped off all their clothes like two young teenage kids. Then Atty started dashing though the wood with Bill chasing her. He really enjoyed the sight of her naked female body in motion – her hands flaying about, her lovely buttock gyrating, and her breasts bouncing around on her chest.

Then they came into an open area of big rocks, and among them they found a nice grassy spot that was well hidden from view. Bill grasped the naked Atty in his arms, kissed her, and then pulled her down upon the grass. Like a proper gentleman Bill lay on his back directly on the grass and let Atty lie on top of him.

Of course, they made love on the grassy spot, and then snoozed in the warm sun despite the elevation. Finally, they arose and started back to where they left their clothes, hand and hand and laughing. Bill did not realize how far they had run naked through the wood, but luckily he remembered where they had left their clothes.

Suddenly, however, they were shocked by the sound of laughter and voices coming from down the hill, not too far away! This was terrible! They were two very adult and respectable people – but they were shark naked in the middle of the woods! It would be horrible if they were caught without a stich of clothes.

Since they would not be able to reach their clothes before the people arrived, Bill quickly found another thicket in which they could hide. The people kept coming closer and closer, and Bill and Atty cowered in fear of being discovered. It would be so horrible.

Then the people, several adults, some teenagers, and some children came right by to the thicket where Bill and Atty were hiding. The lovers could see the people quite clearly and even make out their faces. But they were not sure whether the visitors could see them in the thicket! Fortunately, however, the people passed right on by without discovering the naked pair.

They waited until the people were well gone and their noise was receding in the distance. Then they carefully strode to the spot where their clothes were concealed, and quickly got dressed. The fear of being discovered naked now turned to elation for their "salvation"! They embraced in "triumph" and then kissed, and then they had a good laugh about the whole incident.

"What would your father and the Dutch government say if you were found naked in the woods with an American sailor?" Bill teased Atty.

"What would the President of the United States say if you were found naked in the woods with a foreign girl?" Atty countered.

He responded by giving her a kiss, and then they walked hand and hand down off the mountain to the Lodge.

It was already in the afternoon, and they needed some nourishment after their "great adventure". As a precaution when the lovers entered the restaurant of the Lodge, Atty went first to check on the occupants. Then she suddenly stopped, frozen in her step.

"Oh, my goodness!" she exclaimed! "It's my father!"

Atty started backing out of the doorway, signaling Bill not to enter. But she was recognized by one of her father's associates, and they all turned to look at her.

"Disappear! Go to the cabin!" Atty whispered to Bill since he had not yet been spotted, and then Atty walked boldly into the restaurant.

Bill quickly left the area and headed down to the cabin. He waited there impatiently wondering what Atty was going through. Did her father suspect that his daughter was up here with him? Anything could be happening up there in the restaurant – he would just have to wait and see!

Actually, it wasn't too long before Atty finally did come down to the cabin. She was smiling.

"My father doesn't trust me," she exclaimed. "I explained that I just wanted a few days off by myself, but I don't think he believes me. He is still suspicious." Then she added more determinedly, "Anyway, I am a big girl now, over thirty, and I can do what I want."

"Of course you are," Bill reassured her."

"He is long gone now, let's get something to eat," Atty added.

Just to be sure that her father would not pop back to the lodge, however, Atty suggested that they get a snack at a food stand in a small village down the hill. Accordingly, they walked down the steps to the village below the lodge. After having some snacks, they then spent the rest afternoon wandered through the village and looking in all the gift shops.

It was almost dark by the time by the time that they got back to the cabin. They quickly cleaned up and then headed up to the Lodge. Atty checked with the staff of the Lodge and confirmed that her father had not come back, so they sat down to dinner.

Again, they had a very romantic dinner with candlelight and wine. Then they followed it with coffee and brandy for Bill and tea for Atty. Afterwards, they went down the steps to their cabin, where Bill built a nice big fire in the fireplace and Atty moved the big soft chair in front.

They both undressed and Atty sat back in the chair while Bill knell on the floor in front of her. Then they made love like before!

The two lovers remained there in front of the fire afterwards for a long time before going to bed. Then they cuddled as they went to sleep.

The next morning they bathed together again as before. Then they got dressed and they went up to the Lodge for a breakfast.

Atty had prearranged that a car and driver would pick them that morning, and they started down from Puncak Pass. Soon the tea plantations disappeared, the little villages passed by, and then they among the rice fields again. They drove right through Bogor and onward to Batavia.

Atty dropped Bill off at the airport and then headed back to her house. And Bill caught a naval shuttle back to Surabaya.

16

"Well, lover boy," Phil greeted Bill jovially as Bill reported in. "I am afraid "papa" has been asking after you!" Bill was quite surprised! "Yes, a Mr. Vanderpan has been asking about the whereabouts of a Commander Taylor through naval channels. I just happened to report that such naval officer was on a ship and out to sea."

Bill thanked his old friend, and his commanding officer, for making an excuse about his whereabouts. My goodness, Bill though, Atty's father was really suspicious! This might cause problems in the future.

"Well, it was almost true since we are heading out this afternoon." Phil advised, "You had better get back to your ship!"

According to Phil, his Destroyer Division was to first sail to Tjilatjap on the south coast of Java, and then escort some ships to Darwin in Australia. That afternoon, instead of returning to the Java Sea the four destroyers headed out through the Madura Strait between Java and Madura, and continued into the Bali Strait until they reached the Indian Ocean. Again, while there were no Japanese surface warships in the Indian Ocean, there was always the danger of Japanese submarines seeking to attack the Allied supply lines.

Sailing westward along the southern coast of Java they finally reached Tjilatjap the next morning. This was the only significant port on the south coast of Java, and quite a busy one. The city itself is perched on a steep hillside, but it was not very attractive. Indeed, the waterfront was dominated by industrial types of buildings, unlike the more pleasant Surabaya.

The destroyers picked up the various ships in the port, and the convoy turned east toward Darwin. After passing through the Indian Ocean, the convoy entered the Timor Sea before finally reaching Darwin. The trip to Darwin took two days.

It was quite a bustling city, the only one in the sparsely settled northern area of Australia. Many Australian troops had been transferred there during the previous year to defend the northern part of the country in case of a Japanese attack on Australia.

The destroyers then returned to Surabaya after a two days run, arriving back on January 15th.

Upon arriving back in port Bill and the other destroyer division crew heard the bad news that Japan finally invaded the Dutch East Indies. Several days earlier they captured Manado on the far northern part of Celebes Island. This was the city near where Allied planes attacked the *Pope* when they were coming south from the Philippines. It had no oil deposits but apparently the Japanese wanted to use it as an air base to strike deeper into the East Indies.

Then a day later the Japanese captured the oil center of Tarakan in north Borneo, the city where Bill's division visited just a short time ago. The Dutch destroyed as much as possible before evacuating the place.

In response to the invasion of the Dutch East Indies the Allies were now joining together in a combined military defense force. It was a rather belated effort and probably should have been done shortly after the war with Japan started. Undoubtedly, people knew very well that Japan probably would be coming after the oil reservoirs in Borneo.

Now the American, British, Dutch, and Australian military forces were being combined into the "ABDA" Command with headquarters in Bandung. This was the city in the mountains of West Java where the Dutch were planning to move the capital from Batavia. The British Field Marshall Sir Archibald Wavell was placed in overall command of the Allied forces, while the American Admiral Hart was placed in overall command of combined naval forces. His authority over the Dutch and British ships, however, really did not exist at all.

Admiral Glassford, meanwhile, was directly in charge of the American ships. Generally the Americans were responsible for the eastern zone from Surabaya to New Guinea. The British were responsible from Singapore west to Ceylon, whereas the Dutch were responsible for the central area in between, around Sumatra and Java.

The US Asiatic Fleet was still headquartered in Surabaya with Admiral Hart overall in command of all components of the fleet. Admiral Glassford was still the commander of Task Force 5, which consisted of all the surface ships of the fleet.

17

Bill also received a message that arrived at the Destroyer Squadron headquarters. It was from a nurse at a Dutch medical clinic in Surabaya with the message that he should contact them at a specific number. When Bill tried the number he reached a nurse who, after he identified himself, asked him to wait one moment.

"Hello, Admiral Darling," Atty's sweet voice greeted him. Bill was happy to hear from her. And he particularly overjoyed when she announced that she was now staying with some girlfriends in Surabaya. She asked him to meet her at the main gate to the navy base.

Bill hurried back to his quarters, advised Henry where he was going, and then rushed to the gate. Atty was there waiting for him at the gate with a car and driver. He jumped into the back seat, and they hugged and kissed. Then Atty motioned to the Javanese driver to proceed.

Bill asked about her fiancé, Hans. Atty happily reported that he went to Australia and will be gone for a long, long time. As they rode along Atty explained that Hans had been promoted to a new diplomatic position and that he had been transferred to Australia permanently. Any martial prospects they had were thereby indefinitely postponed.

Atty also mentioned that here in East Java the people spoke Javanese as different from Sundanese in West Java. Only the better educated Javanese could speak the new Indonesian language, and some even Dutch, but normally they used their "mother tongue" in their family and among themselves. Atty herself could only speak Indonesian or Sundanese, but not Javanese.

The car proceeded to a higher elevation in the city and into a rich residential area. Finally they pulled into the courtyard of a very elegant mansion and were greeted by the Javanese jaga, or guard. Then two young and pretty Dutch girls burst eagerly out of the house, and greeted them as Bill and Atty got out of the car. .

"So this is your Admiral Darling!" the younger of them exclaimed merrily in English as she surveyed Bill up and down. "Yes," she addressed Bill with a big smile! "If you get tired of that old lady, you can try me instead!" She finished with a laugh, kissed him on his cheek, and spoke in Dutch to Atty.

"Oh, yes," the other girl chimed in, "he is really quite cute! Where did you find him, Atty?" She shook Bill's hand rather than kiss him. Atty responded to both of the girls in Dutch.

Then the two young girls grabbed Bill by his arms and led him into the house. Atty followed complaining to the girls in Dutch. The house had a beautiful view down upon the city and out over the waterfront and the harbor.

Once inside Atty introduced Bill to her girlfriends, who were sisters and both who were younger than Atty. The elder one was Susanne, or Sue for short. She was married and her husband was in Australia for the time being. The younger girl, the one that spoke first, was Juliana or Juli for short. She was unmarried, and she was still looking a husband Atty joked. Atty assured Bill that the sisters were quite close friends of hers from way back in Holland, and both of them would keep their mouths shut about him.

It being already late in the afternoon, and the four of them sat on the veranda of the big house with a beautiful view out over the harbor of Surabaya with Madura Island in the background. They had a number of drinks together until dinner time.

The sisters had prepared a nice Dutch-Indonesian dinner once they knew that Bill was coming. They had a nice long meal, with wine and a lot of chatting. It was followed by coffee and brandy, and tea and after-dinner drinks!

They all had a good time together, but then Atty said it was time for bed – even though it was still early. The sisters giggled, but Atty led Bill out of the main house to the separate guest house. She was staying there, she complained jokingly, because the sisters made too much noise for her.

Atty led Bill into the guest house and then locked the door after her, smiling at Bill mischievously. She then embraced him and kissed him.

"It's been a week!" Atty declared with some exaggeration. "Are you going to rape me?"

With this she pulled Bill over to the bed, and she backed onto it, pulling him right along with her! Lying beside her, Bill pulled the top of Atty's dress open and revealed her bra-clad breasts! He then literally tore the bra open to expose her breasts, which he grasped with both hands and handled them lustfully!

Atty did not resist but instead stretched her arms above her head to let him have his way with her! In response Bill lowered his head between her breasts and then proceeded to suck her nipples – one breast at time!

Bill then pulled Atty's dress down and took it completely off her body! Then he quickly followed with her panties! Stripping off his own clothes he rolled naked atop of her body again and rubbed his male body on her female form!

Bill spread her legs apart and he soon entered her body! Then he proceeded to make love to her while Atty responded in kind! They continued their love making until they had a nice orgasm!

Then they just lay there together with Bill's head up on her abdomen, her fingers slowly running through his hair, lightly massaging his head. In time, however, they stirred, crawled into the bed covers, and cuddled as they went to sleep.

When Bill awoke early in the morning, Atty had already drawn her bath and was sitting in it. He joined her and they bathed each other. Finally, they dressed and joined the two girls for breakfast.

"Did you have a nice night?" naughty Juli asked, and both girls giggled. Atty scolded them in Dutch as if she was the mother hen. Then they all sat down for breakfast together.

"We have decided to hold a nice dinner party for some of your officer friends tonight," Juli announced with a big smile. "Could you persuade some of them to join us?"

"Of course I could. I could persuade the whole US Navy to come!" Bill declared excitedly. "How many would you like?"

"Oh, the more the merrier," Juli gushed, "I like men!" Both her sister Sue and Atty scolded Juli in Dutch for being so "promiscuous".

"Just a couple of officers," Sue stated trying to be more serious. "We were thinking of a more formal dinner. We just love to see you men in your pretty uniforms! They make you look so handsome!"

Bill thought for a moment, and then replied.

"Well, I have three fellow skippers," Bill ventured, "and one commanding officer. And with my exec whom Atty has already met, that would be six counting me. Is that too many?"

"Oh no, perfect!" Juli exclaimed eagerly! "That's two men for every woman! That's a beautiful arrangement!" Atty and Sue both chided young Juli in Dutch, but they both merrily accepted the number!

In fact, Sue added, "Remember we want to see you fellows all dressed up in your pretty uniforms!" Bill promised compliance, and they all had a laugh.

Bill then bide the two sisters goodbye, and rode with Atty down to the gate. Bill mentioned how glad the men would be to be able to socialize with women again. At the gate to the base, Atty kissed him goodbye.

Bill immediately went into his Division headquarters. When he walked in Phil and the other three skippers were present and he was greeted with a mixture of sarcastic and envious comments.

"Well, welcome back to the Navy, lover boy!" one of the fellows teased Bill. This was followed by other comments about his love life involving a girl and not his ship!

"Well, I guess you guys would not be interested in the fact that three pretty Dutch girls have invited my fellow ship captains and commanding officer to a dinner party in their house tonight!" Bill responded to them in an apologetic voice.

Immediately there was a hush in the room as they all looked at Bill with open mouths! After all, most of them had not socialized with females since the dependents had been sent back to the States, or since arriving from the States, except the few who had fooled around with Filipino girls!

"Oh, yes we would be!" Al declared as he broke the silence. And the other officers quickly seconded Phil's declaration.

"Are the other two as pretty as your girlfriend?" Al continued, as he was one of the skippers who one had already met Atty before. Then he turned to the other guys, "Bill's girlfriend is an absolute knockout!"

"Almost," Bill declared! "They are really cute – and younger! Of course, it may be too much trouble for you guys to wear dress whites for the occasion!"

"Wait a moment!" the others suddenly burst out! The mood had now changed from one of amused sarcasm to one of eager anticipation and fawning over Bill!

"Yes, yes, we want to go!" Then they discussed the details of when and what. And Phil, Bill's superior and close friend, was also all smiles.

"Now be sure to behave yourselves," Bill warned them, "they are very proper upper class ladies!"

The men eagerly agreed, and rushed out to their quarters or ships to get their dress whites cleaned and pressed. While they performed various duties on their ships, all thoughts were focused on the dinner party that night with the pretty Dutch girls.

Meanwhile, Bill also invited Henry to come along, and he too was excited. When the officers dressed in their dress white uniforms, everyone asked where they going in their formal dress. But they refused to reveal anything.

Phil arranged to get a military sedan from the base to supplement the car Atty sent down to pick up Bill. The men, all specked and spanned, gathered at the front gate. At the appointed time, the car from Atty arrived, and Bill, Phil, and Henry climbed in while the other three officers rode in the other vehicle. Then both vehicles were driven up to the Dutch girls' house.

They arrived in the mansion courtyard and were let into the foyer by one of the servants. Atty then came out to greet them in her flashing manner, dressed in a formal and flowing gown! All the men were stunned in silence as they beheld her!

"Wow!" Phil muttered almost to himself, "What a beautiful woman!" The other men had a similar reaction, even Henry and Al, both of whom had met Atty before!

Then the two sisters appeared, both as pretty as a picture in their formal gowns. The five men stood silent as Bill introduced each one to the girls, Phil first since he was the superior officer. The men only slowly unwound as they were each introduced. By the time all the introductions were made, the men were all smiles.

Atty grabbed Bill and Phil by their arms and led them into the big living room. The two sisters each took two of the other officers and followed. The men were offered drinks at the bar manned by a pretty Javanese girl. Juli served as the translator since the latter, of course, could not understand English.

After a few drinks the male visitors were quite relaxed and chatted freely with the girls. Atty, as the senior hostess, made sure that each of the officers was made comfortable, but the other girls were eager to do their part as well.

Finally a loud gong rang from the other room, and the girls each grabbed two men and led them into a large dining room.

The seating was prearranged with Bill and Phil at the two ends, and the females distributed do that a man was seated on either side of them, and all the men had at least a woman on one side of them.

Atty then announced that they would be having a Rijsttafel, a Dutch word for a special Dutch-Indonesian meal. Bill had already experienced it at the fancy restaurant in Menteng when he visited Atty in Batavia. He warned the men to eat slowly and carefully since they would be served dish after dish in an almost endless manner.

The men all laughed, but then they were pleasantly surprised when six pretty Indonesian girls, dressed in Javanese national costume, came bearing plates of the first course. They stood smiling behind the table until signaled by Sue, the older sister and the chief organizer of the dinner. Then the girls served the six men first – since they were the guests in the female household.

This was followed with more and more dishes, accompanied by wine or beer as the men chose. Despite Bill's warning his fellow sailors ate too much at each serving, and in due course none of them could eat anything more. Coffee and tea, and brandy and other after dinner drinks were served liberally. They all sat at the table for a long time, talking, laughing, and telling jokes.

Finally the dinner came to an end, and the officers, except for Bill, thanked the girls for such a wonderful time, and then bide them a fond goodbye. Bill promised Phil that he would be back early in the morning. This time no one blamed him for his amorous adventures, and the other men climbed into the two cars and returned to the base.

It was Bill's turn now to thank the girls for putting on such a wonderful dinner for his fellow officers. Then he and Atty retired to the guest house for the night. Once in the room they embraced and kissed.

"Be sure to hang up your pretty uniform nice and neat," Atty instructed him as she turned away from him to remove some of her jewelry. Obediently, he shed his shoes and socks, and then removed his dress whites and carefully hung them up. Atty turned back and looked at Bill, clad only in his undershorts.

"Your shorts …" Atty continued with a laugh as she pointed downward with her finger, "… off!"

Bill removed his shorts, but felt kind of silly standing there completely naked in front of Atty who was fully dressed in a beautiful gown. She walked over to him and turned with her back to him.

"Unzip my dress please … and be careful with it!" Atty directed him. But instead Bill clutched her tightly from behind, grabbed hold of breasts with his hands, and pressed his naked body against her gowned body!

"Stop that!" she complained! "Unzip my dress … please!"

After having his fun, Bill proceeded to unzip her gown and then lowered the dress so that Atty could step out of it. He patted her panty-clad buttocks in the process. Then she turned, put her arms around his neck, pressed her bra-clad breasts into his bare chest and thrust her panty-clad pelvis against his naked pelvis.

“Now do you think you can undo my brassiere without damaging it like you did last night?” Atty asked him with a giggle.

Bill assured her he could, and quickly he unfastened the garment. Atty let the garment fall, and then pressed her bare breasts tightly into his naked chest. At the same time she rubbed her panty-clad pelvis against his bare sexual organ, wiggling it back and forth, making sure his manhood was fully enlarged!

“And now my panties!” She directed him!

Bill reached down and hooked his thumbs into the waistband of Atty’s panties. Then as he lowered himself and pulled the garment down, he sucked each of her nipples as he fell on his knees! Then he pulled the panties all the way down to her legs and pulled the garment completely off her feet!

“Kiss me!” she demanded!

Obediently, Bill grasped Att’s naked body in his arms and gave her a long passionate kiss! Then he carried her over to the bed, laid her on her back and lay down beside her. He gently massaged her naked body with his hand and played with her breasts until she pulled his head to her bosom! Then he sucked on her nipples as he climbed between her legs!

Bill entered her body and proceeded to make love to her! He continued until they were both sexually satisfied! Finally they cuddled in bed and went to sleep.

Early in the morning Bill had a funny dream. He dreamt that he was lying on his back on the bed naked and spread-eagled! Juliana was giggling as she was holding his arms up above his head, and Susanna was holding his feet wide apart! Atty, meanwhile, was naked and mounted on top of him! She had taken his manhood into her body, and was proceeding to "rape" him!

As he awoke, Bill realized that his dream was partially true. Juli and Sue were not there of course, but Atty was! And she was mounted on top of him, his hardened member was inserted into her body, and she was making love to him! Bill groaned in sexual enjoyment and started to move!

"Lie at attention, sailor, don't move a muscle!" Atty ordered him! "I am raping you!"

Bill obviously had no objections to being "raped" by a sexy woman, and he just lay there as motionless as possible – under the highly sexually stimulating circumstances! It really was a most enjoyable way to have sex! But Atty's actions were so strong that he did not "last" long, and she soon brought his tense body to a sexual climax! Bill had an orgasm and then fell back sexually used!

Atty could tell immediately that her lover was spent but she kept "raping" him until he went completely limp! Then she gave him a nice long kiss!

Afterward, they bathed together as usual, and then got dressed. When Bill and Atty came to the main house, Bill was wearing his navy dress whites. The two sisters said how handsome he looked.

Bill had breakfast, and then Atty drove him down to the base. They embraced, kissed, and said goodbye!

18

Bill quickly changed clothes and then reported in at the Destroyer Squadron headquarters in time for the officers' call. All the destroyer skippers present in Surabaya at the time were in attendance. It was now January 17th, and Captain Warner, commander of Destroyer Squadron 29 gave the briefing.

The intelligence reports were now indicating that since the Japanese had already taken Tarakan in northern Borneo, they were gathering an invasion force to move into the Makassar Strait between Borneo and Celebes, and threatening to attack the much richer oil city of Balikpapan.

Since this was in the American theater of operations Admiral Hart ordered Admiral Glassford to gather an American naval force to intercept the Japanese invasion. The Americans ships were scattered at the moment, but most of them were ordered to assemble at Kebola Bay on Sumbara Island, just over three hundred miles east of Surabaya.

Bill called Atty to let her know that he would be gone for a while. Then he returned to the *Pope* and informed his officers of the plans for the operation. The officers, and the rest of the crew, were excited to finally be able to battle the Japanese navy rather than just perform boring and unexciting convoy duty.

Indeed, since the war started a month and a half ago, the American surface warships had spent all there time escorting convoys. This new action now was intended to be the first engagement, for which they had been trained, with the Japanese navy. And they all looked forward to it.

Phil's division of destroyers, including the *John D. Ford*, the *Pope*, the *Parrott*, and the *Paul Jones*, left Surabaya that afternoon. They arrived at Sumbara Island the next day. The heavy cruiser *Houston*, and the light cruisers *Marblehead* and *Boise*, as well as Destroyer Division 58 with another four ships, were soon assembled there together with Phil's four destroyers.

Admiral Glassford called all the skippers together and outlined the plan of attack. The *Marblehead* and the eight destroyers were to lead in a night torpedo attack on the Japanese force as it entered the Makassar Strait. The *Houston* and *Boise* would remain some fifty miles south of the strike force to cover the withdrawal of the destroyers as might be required.

But as the ships were refueling to move out the next day, reports came in to indicate that the Japanese force was not headed toward Makassar Strait. So instead the American force stood down and began to return to other duties on the following day. Phil's four destroyers headed back to Surabaya.

But the Destroyer Division 59 had hardy reached port in Surabaya when Admiral Hart ordered them to report back to the rendezvous at Sumbara Island. Apparently, a Japanese force was now reported to be definitely heading to the Makassar Strait.

When Phil and the other destroyer skippers arrived back at Sumbara, the American force was now limited to the

Marblehead, the *Boise,* and just six destroyers. But soon tragedy struck the attack force even before the mission got underway! On its way to the rendezvous the *Boise*, the modern light cruiser, struck an uncharted rock and gashed a big hole in its hull. It had to retire to the nearest port for temporary repair, and a destroyer was sent to escort it. [It eventually had to return to the States for repair.]

Then the *Marblehead,* the more obsolete light cruiser and Admiral Glassford's flagship, had turbine problems and it too had to retire from the actual attack force. Another destroyer had to remain with it to protect from it from a submarine attack. The *Marblehead* would now instead just provide fire support for the withdrawing destroyers. Admiral Glassford, on the *Marblehead,* was still technically in command of the operation, but it limped far behind the destroyers.

It was now left to just Commander Phil Tower's Destroyer Division 59, with its four destroyers, including Bill's *Pope*, to proceed with the mission. Phil issued his battle orders to the four skippers to use only torpedoes at the enemy transports, engage the warships only if required to complete the mission, and use guns only after all torpedoes were used, or if necessary.

It was in the afternoon of January 23rd when Phil's division headed out from Sumbara Island and crossed the Java Sea to Celebes. He purposely kept his ships close to Celebes to mislead any Japanese planes in case any of them spotted the destroyers. No Japanese planes were encountered, and the only aircraft seen was an American PBY. The *Marblehead*, meanwhile, limped along far behind.

As soon as it was dark, however, the destroyer division turned northwest and headed across the Makassar Strait towards Borneo. As the task force of four destroyers continued up the strait, Bill and his crew were quite excited about finally taking the fight to the enemy.

About midnight the lookouts reported bursts of lights in the sky far ahead. Then there was a strange glow in the sky as they neared Balikpapan. As they got closer it was revealed that several Japanese ships were burning due to American and Dutch bombers that had struck earlier. They purposely avoided these enemy ships in order to prevent detection if at all possible.

By about two-thirty in the morning the destroyers were abreast of Balikpapan and they could clearly see raging fires in and around the city. Apparently the Japanese had already landed at the city and the Dutch were in the process of destroying the oil wells and other facilities before they were captured. Black smoke from the fires spread out some twenty miles into the strait, which incidentally helped to conceal the approaching destroyers.

Indeed, as the destroyers continued onward a large Japanese warship burst right passed them, not suspecting that Allied ships would dare be attacking the Japanese invasion force. Then four Japanese destroyers also passed them but without incident.

Soon the American ships found themselves amid their targets, the Japanese transports. The destroyers began launching torpedoes. The *Pope* fired several torpedoes as did the other destroyers, some at close range, but there were no hits, apparently due to faulty torpedoes.

But the surprise was lost! The torpedoes banging against ships, but not exploding, caused alarm. Light signals flashed and Japanese destroyers came rushing out into the strait. By three o'clock the American destroyers had passed through the whole pack of Japanese transports without scoring one explosion. Phil then signaled the division to turn around again in order to make another run through the ships.

This time the torpedoes began to explode and at least two transports were sunk and others were damaged. The Americans then turned around once more to make third run through the transports. Japanese cruisers and destroyers rushed out into the strait, apparently thinking that they were being attacked by submarines. The destroyers used up their last torpedoes with more hits and sinking Japanese vessels.

Then the destroyers used their guns to blast away at the transports, causing quite a bit of damage. The Japanese, finally realizing that they were being attacked by surface ships, now started returning fire and the John D. Ford was slightly damaged, wounding four men.

Before the Japanese cruisers and destroyers descended on them, however, Phil ordered the division to race out of there, and they left the battle scene as fast as they could. The Americans later reported that they had sunk six ships and damaged many more in the battle.

But they had not stopped the invasion of Balikpapan. Indeed, the Japanese took over the important oil city even while most of the facilities were temporarily damaged.

At dawn the destroyers were far down the Makassar Strait. As it became light they kept a close watch for pursuers, but none appeared. Apparently, the Japanese were too busy rescuing many of their people cast into the sea from the sinking or damaged ships. The American destroyers, meanwhile, crossed the Java Sea and returned to their base in Surabaya, reaching there early morning the following day, January 25th, after an acclaimed victory.

The battle, the first between surface ships of the Asiatic Fleet and the Japanese navy, had been a victory for the Americans. Even if they were lucky not to have to tangle with enemy destroyers or cruisers themselves, the victory greatly lifted the morale of not only the participating crews of the destroyers, but also that of the whole fleet as well.

19

After a good night's sleep lasting well into the morning, Bill finally went over to the Squadron Headquarters to call Atty. It was more than a week since he had last seen her, and he was eager to see her again. Atty had been terribly worried about him, and she persuaded him to join her for lunch at her house. It was agreed that she would come down to pick him up at noon. Bill told her that he could only stay for lunch as he had to be on the base in the afternoon.

Meanwhile, Bill had to look after his ship. Besides refueling, all four destroyers needed refurbishment as well as rearmament. They took turns in the major repair yard while the others rested in the camouflaged destroyer haven. This gave Bill several days to be with Atty again.

He was at the front gate precisely at noon, and Atty showed up with her car and driver shortly afterwards. Bill jumped in the car with Atty and they embraced and kissed each other passionately. After all, it had been more than a week since they were together. He reminded her that he could only stay for lunch, although he might be able to come back that evening.

Atty squeezed his arm as giggled she said that she wanted to give him a special lunch. Once they reached the house Atty took Bill directly to her private guest house rather than the dining room! After locking the door after them, they embraced again and had a long kiss!

She proceeded to unbutton Bill's shirt and removed his shirt, then unbuckled his belt and pulled down his pants! She knelt on the floor in from of him as she took off his shoes and socks, and removed his pants. Then she reached up and pulled down his shorts.

Since Bill was quite excited by now, his hardened manhood jumped out at Atty and almost hit her right in the face!

"What a naughty boy you are!" Atty scolded him as she swatted his "offending member" away!

"Aw shucks," Bill complained disappointedly!

"Behave yourself!" Atty stated bluntly as she rose up on her feet. "Now you can undress me!" Then she pressed against him front to front as she waited for him to unzip the back of her dress.

Bill dutifully zipped down her dress, and unfastened her brassiere. Atty moved away to let both garments fall to the floor. Then she pressed her naked breasts into his bare chest and her panty-clad pelvis into his hardened organ! Bill continued by hooking his thumbs in her panties and began to pull them down.

As he lowered himself to pull down the panties all the way, he sucked on each nipple in turn! Then Bill removed the garments off her feet!

Atty pulled him over to the bed. She laid down on it on her back, and hooking her hands behind her legs she pulled them up over her body and wide apart – fully exposing her womanhood to Bill! She told him to kneel on the bed between her legs!

“All right now, have a nice “lunch”!” Atty giggled as she pulled him onto her! Bill automatically mounted her and proceeded to make love to Atty!

“Hurry! Faster! Harder!” Atty encouraged him, and Bill proceeded as fast and hard as he could! She wrapped her legs around his head, and placed her heels on his bare back! Then when they achieved an orgasm her thighs pressed against his face and her heels scarped his back!

“Good boy!” Atty congratulated him! “Did you enjoy your lunch?” Atty asked lovingly!

“It was wonderful,” Bill responded.

Afterwards they lay there in bed together with Bill’s head lying on Atty’s abdomen while she running her fingers through his hair. In due course they both got up and got dressed. Then she had to run Bill back down to the base but he promised to return that evening.

Bill attended to his ship and his crew that afternoon, but all the time he was thinking of Atty. And his mind particularly centered on the “lunch” she had served him! It was so erotic!

That evening Atty came again with her car and driver. She picked up Bill and they returned to the big house on the hill. She advised him that they would have dinner with the two girls. After a few drinks on the veranda overlooking the bay, the four of them sat down to dinner and enjoyed the food and wine.

It was then that Juliana, the youngest of the two sisters and the unmarried one, asked Bill whether it would be all right to have "Admiral Phil" join them for dinner the next night. She said that she really liked him.

"But he is old enough to be your father!" Bill complained.

"Oh, I like older men – like you!" Juli responded! "Indeed, I would prefer you, but the old hag here has already got you!" This caused Atty to complain to the young girl in Dutch, and Susana to laugh. Anyway, Bill promised to invite Phil for the next night.

After dinner, Atty and Bill finally retired to her guest house. They undressed each other as before, and embracing each other naked they concluded with a nice long kiss.

Then they shifted to the bed and made love in the more normal manner! And in the morning Atty was on top of Bill, humping away for all she was worth! She completely exhausted his sexual powers!

Back at the base, Bill approached Phil. He mentioned that Juliana, the young pretty girl, had specially asked for Phil to come to dinner that night. It was nothing formal, just he and Bill. Phil was surprised. After all, the girl was young enough to be his daughter. And besides that, he was married.

But then … so what! He certainly was flattered, and it was nice having female companionship. He gladly agreed to come.

That evening Atty sent the car down by the driver to pick up the two men. Back up at the house, Juli was quite gracious to Phil, and Bill could see that Phil quite enjoyed it. The five of them had drinks on the veranda, a casual dinner together, and then followed with brandy and coffee and tea, and a lot of talk.

It was then that Julianne stated that the three girls, together with help from some addition Dutch wives, wanted to throw a "garden party" for the American officers.

This would include more men than just the ship captains, and after discussing numbers it was finally decided that there could be five men from each ship. With Phil, that would be twenty-one sailors, quite a crowd! And it would have to begin tomorrow at two o'clock, and dress whites were required. Phil and Bill happily agreed, and stated that their selected men would love it.

Then at an appropriate time, Susana excused herself and went to her room. That was a signal for Atty and Bill to slip off to the guest house, and Phil and Juli were left alone.

In the guest house the two lovers quickly undressed, climbed naked on the bed together and made love! Early in the morning, Atty woke Bill on top of him in the usual manner!

When they returned to the main house, the other three were already up having breakfast. Then the car took Bill and Phil down to the base. Despite Bill's prodding, Phil refused to divulge what Juli and he did the previous night after Bill and Atty left. Phil remarked that a gentleman doesn't talk about such things.

The refurbishment of the four destroyers was to be completed that day, and they would be back on Convoy duty the next day. Phil had to look after the needs for the whole Division, while Bill had check on the *Pope*, which was now ready for duty again.

But meantime, each of the skippers had to pick four of their men to join them for the special garden party that afternoon. Bill selected Henry, as his executive officer, and Lieutenant Mike Worthington, his gunnery officer. Then to spread the "happiness" lower among the ranks, he selected Ensign Roberts and Chief Petty Officer Benson. Chief Benson was particularly appreciative since he was not a regular officer, only a non-commissioned officer, but he and Bill knew each other from way back.

Bill went up the house at noon time before the others to check on the preparations of the garden party. He was surprised to find a lot of Javanese helpers rigging up large canvases outside the house to provide shelter from the hot tropic sun. And the main house was also being set up for a large party as well.

But Atty, with a giggle, dragged Bill off to the guest house for "lunch"! Laughingly she undressed Bill first since she did not want to get his pretty uniform messy. Then as he stood there completely naked she embraced and kissed him while she had him undress her!

As usual Bill sucked her nipples and kissed her *mons veneris* as he removed her bra and panties! Then as Atty spread her legs wide apart he ducked his head between her thighs and gave her an intimate kiss!

Then Atty quickly jumped on the bed, laid on her back, pulled up her legs wide apart! Bill obediently positioned himself between her thighs, and made love to her again!

Afterwards, the couple slowly got dressed and then joined the preparations for the garden party. The place was already transformed with a formal bar set up in the living room as well as long food tables. Javanese servants were running all over the place under the direction of Sue, Juli, and three new Dutch wives, one who was young and pretty.

By two o'clock in the afternoon when the preparations were complete, it was also time for the Americans officers to arrive. Atty had sent a car down to lead the way, and Phil had arranged to get several other vehicles to transport all the men.

When they pulled up in the courtyard Bill and Atty went on the big porch to greet them. Atty wore a particularly nice dress, and the men who had not met her before were awed by her appearance. No wonder Bill went way out of his way, they thought, and seriously bent navy regulations to be with her. Any red-blooded man would do the same!

Soon, Susanna, Julianne, and the other three Dutch women also came out onto the porch, and now the men had six females to look at.

Phil went up onto the porch, and as the superior officer he handled the introduction of the men. Actually, he introduced the captains of each ship, whom the three girls had already met at the dinner party, and then each captain introduced the men they had invited from their ship. Bill was last, and he introduced Henry and Ensign Roberts, who already had meet Atty, and then Mike and Chief Benson who had not.

Then it was Atty's turn as being the chief woman present. She welcomed the men to the Dutch East Indies, to Surabaya, to the house, and to the garden party. She then introduced the Dutch women, including Sue, Juli, and the other young Dutch girl, Georgia, as well as the two older Dutch wives. Atty announced that the latter would serve drinks at the bar while each of the four younger women would be the "hostess" of each ship, she being that of Bill's ship. Then she bide them all to enter, get drinks, have something to eat, and enjoy themselves at the garden party.

Needless to say, the men did just that! They were all enthralled with the decorated house and garden, the Dutch ladies, and a host of young Javanese servants who were scurrying about. It was completely in contrast to their quarters on their ships or in the Surabaya barracks. They had drinks, ate the food, and flirted with the girls – if they had a chance. After all, there were five men for every young Dutch girl.

But then, there were also a number of pretty Javanese girls as well.

The party went on for the rest of the afternoon and early evening, and everyone enjoyed themselves, the women as well as the men. But when darkness set it was time for the officers to return to their ships as they had to prepare for their departure in the morning. Atty and Bill rode in the last car down to the base, and after the others climbed out of the vehicle, Atty delayed Bill's departure.

She grabbed him and embraced him tightly, almost weeping as if this was their last goodbye. They kissed passionately. Then Bill had to depart, and he sadly watched the car drive off.

20

The skippers of the destroyers all meet with Phil in the division headquarters later than evening. They thanked Bill, as well as Phil, for the wonderful time that they and their men had that afternoon. They could not stop talking about the event, and particularly about all the lovely ladies. And they kept saying how lucky Bill for have such a beautiful girlfriend.

But then they got down to business. One bit of shocking news was that the US Navy Department had suddenly "deactivated" the Asiatic Fleet under Admiral Hart and instead formed a new Southwest Pacific Command under Admiral Glassford. This caused a great confusion since Admiral Hart was still the commander of the ships in the "deactivated" fleet, which were the same ships under Admiral Glassford's command. Needless to say, despite the Navy Department's confused arrangement, the hierarchy in the American fleet stayed pretty much the same for the time being.

But more pressing was then fact that the Japanese had been pushing southward through the Dutch East Indies. They had already occupied Balikpapan on eastern Borneo, as the skippers knew first hand, and soon afterward they captured Kentari in southeast Celebes in the Banda Sea. Also, Ambon on Maluku Islands, where Bill spent New Year's Eve with Atty, was captured. Both of these latter were not oil cities, but it brought the Japanese farther south and closer to Java itself.

The current task for Destroyer Division 59 was to escort ships from southern Celebes and Borneo, particularly the big city of Makassar in southern Celebes and Banjarmasin, the Dutch capital on Borneo, and bring them to Batavia. The Dutch intended to withdraw everything to Java in order to make a last stand there.

On the morning of January 28th the four ships of Destroyer Division 59 sailed out of Surabaya northeastward across the Java Sea. They reached Makassar early the next morning. Like Surabaya, Makassar was a rather pretty city. And while it was not an oil city, it had a large functioning airport. Now it was being cleared out and left with only a small defending Dutch army.

The destroyers escorted the ships that were capable of leaving, on a last chance basis, out of Makassar and headed westward to Banjarmasin, the Dutch capital of Borneo on the south coast. It was reached later that night. It too was being cleared out of as much as possible.

The next morning the convoy headed southwest to Tanjung-Priok, the port of Batavia, where they reached the next day. The port was filled with ships, many refugees from the northern ports. The destroyers then headed eastward to their home port of Surabaya, which they reached the following night.

21

On the morning of the 1st of February, Bill called Atty that he was back "home" for a few days. He was eager to see her and made arrangements to visit her that noon. He was eager to have lunch with her as before.

Atty meet him with the car and driver, and they embraced and kissed in the back seat of the car. Then they drove up to the house, and quickly slipped into the guest house.

They stripped each other, and Bill eagerly sucked on her nipples and kissed her between her thighs! Then Atty jumped on the bed pulling her legs up and far apart! After kissing her again, he proceeded to make love to her!

After making love to her, Bill laid his head on her abdomen as she ran her fingers through his hair. It was so peaceful.

But then suddenly there was a loud pounding on the door, and Juli's voice called out in a panic in Dutch! Atty sat up abruptly!

"It's my father!" Atty almost screamed! "He is in Surabaya, here, and he is coming to the house now!"

Atty jumped out of bed and reached for her clothes, and Bill followed!

"Quick, get dressed!" Atty pleaded with him in a rush! "You need to leave here before he arrives!" Without a word of protest Bill jumped into his clothes, but then he turned to confront Atty.

"This is silly," Bill complained, "it's about time that your father was told about us!"

"Oh, please, darling," Atty pleaded. "Please don't cause a problem. We Dutch are more family-oriented than you Americans. I greatly disappointed my parents when I ran away and married my first husband. I don't want to hurt them again – at least not now!"

Bill tried to argue with her but Atty was determined and begged him to not create a scene. He finally gave up and agreed to leave. Atty escorted him out to the car, they embraced and kissed, and he climbed into her car and left.

It was just in time! As soon as Bill's car pulled around the corner away from the house, he noticed another car coming toward him. Bill screened his face as the cars passed each other, but he recognized Atty's father in the other car.

Bill, meanwhile, thought how absurd the whole thing was. It felt like some high school boy caught kissing a girl and her father chasing after him. But now he was a grown man, over forty years old, the captain of a ship in the United States Navy. It was so ridiculous – just for the love of a woman! But then, of course, Atty was a woman who was really worth everything!

When he got back to the base he called Atty see what was happening with her father. She expanded that her father had gotten wind of the girls' garden party for the American officers from his Dutch naval sources, and that he was furious! He planned to stay around for a few days to check on the situation. Atty urged Bill to get back to his ship in a hurry since her father might get the Dutch navy command to check on whether he was there.

Indeed, it was not too long before a Dutch Admiral with some staff and Mr. Vanderpan himself came to the ship asking after Bill. Atty's father complained to Bill about the garden party, which he assumed that Bill had set it up. While, of course, Bill acknowledged his role to some extent, he tried to downplay the whole event.

Nevertheless, Mr. Vanderpan again stated that he did not Bill to have anything more to do with his daughter. In fact, he was going to take steps to prevent it. Then he turned to the admiral and they seemingly argued in Dutch.

Bill was angry and he was tempted to tell Atty's father about the love affair he and his daughter were having. But then he thought of Atty, and he did not want to hurt her. So he just kept silent.

As soon as they left, Bill went over the squadron headquarters from where he could call Atty. She laughed when he told her that her father had just visited the base with a Dutch admiral to reprimand him. Atty told him that she had to be with her father that evening but that he was leaving tomorrow afternoon. She suggested that they secretly meet for a late afternoon snack today at a restaurant downtown that she named.

So Bill arranged to get a navy vehicle later in the day, and at the appointed time he drove himself downtown. It was the first time he actually drove in Java. It was weird driving on the left side of the road, particularly with the different kinds of traffic all over the road, but he soon got used to it. He found the kafi that Atty had mentioned, and then spotted her standing in front of it.

Bill stopped but instead of having him park Atty instead jumped into the car beside him. They kissed, and she directed him to drive along the waterfront to a special seafood restaurant that she liked. Actually, it was a very crude restaurant specializing in shrimp and crabs. The décor was minimal as was the furniture, but they served lots of fresh shrimp.

Indeed, after they sat down a table, some Javanese workers rolled a barrel right in the front door and through the restaurant and into the kitchen. Atty explained that the barrel contained shrimp that was being delivered directly from a fishing ship. There wasn't a way to get shrimp any fresher than that!

Then when Bill went to the restroom, he had to pass right through the kitchen, and avoid the crabs that were crawling around alive on the floor. Nevertheless, the shrimps were delicious and Atty taught Bill how to eat them by pinching the shell off their backs. And they had a lovely time together.

Atty then suggested a drive along the pretty marina to observe the sights. Bill pulled out and got onto the marina drive.

While he was observing the scenery, Atty leaned over and unzipped Bill's pants and reached in to pull out his male organ, which quickly hardened in the process!

"What are you doing?" Bill asked in puzzlement.

"You take care of the driving," Atty responded with a giggle, "and I'll take care of the driver!"

Then she lowered her head to his lap!

While he was driving along the road and supposedly observing the scenery, it was hard for him to concentrate, particularly with the thrill Atty was giving him!

Atty was nice a neat about it, but as she raised up she was startled to see that she had gotten lipstick on his fly! Then she had a good laugh!

"What are people going to say?" Atty giggled! Bill looked down in horror at his lipstick-smudged pants!

She made Bill stop in a remote place in a park. She walked around to his side of the car, and when he swung around in the driver's seat she used water and tissues to try to wipe off her lipstick from his fly – but with only limited success!

"Oh, just be careful!" Atty laughed. But then she made Bill get out the car as well and pulled him over to a park table.

"Now, I think you should thank me!" she chortled as she pulled off her panties, and jumped up on the edge of the table. She lifted up her dress and spread her legs far apart to fully expose her womanhood!

"All right, Admiral Darling!" Atty chortled again as pointed down between her thighs! "Now be a gentleman!"

Bill dutifully gave her a nice kiss! Then he proceeded to make love to her! It wasn't long before they reached a climax! Then as they had an orgasm and were sexually satisfied, Atty fell flat back on the table!

Bill pulled her up from the table, and kissed her. As they climbed back in the car, Atty laughingly asked him whether he enjoyed his outing. He replied in the affirmative. And she then cuddled up to him and kissed him as he was driving.

Bill dropped Atty off where he had picked her up, and after a kiss she warned him laughingly to look after his pants! Then more seriously, she said she would leave a message when her farther left tomorrow.

When Bill got back to the base he had to use his hat to cover the lipstick stains on the fly of his pants! It was quite awkward but he managed to get back to his quarters without embarrassing himself, and then he quickly changed into another pair of pants.

Bill had plenty to do on the ship, even though Henry was good second officer. Nevertheless, he kept thinking about Atty and was anxious to be with her again! But it was not until the next afternoon that a messenger came from the Squadron headquarters to tell him that the "the bird has flown the coup"! Bill went to the headquarters and called to have her car come down right away.

Indeed, Atty was in the car when it arrived, and she met him with hugs and kisses! On the way back to the house she said that she was going to provide him with a "belated lunch"! Bill just laughed and kissed her.

Up in the house Atty immediately took Bill to the guest house, and locked the door. She embraced him and gave him a long kiss. Then she made him stand still while she undressed him. When he was completely naked, Atty had him undress her, which he did with a relish! He unfastened her dress, and then her bra! She was now clad only panties and heels!

"Now don't be a naughty boy!" Atty exclaimed teasingly! When Bill move toward her, she laughingly ran away! Bill chased after her and Atty scrambled away yelling "Rape, rape, rape!"! Bill, of course, quickly caught her, cast her onto the bed, and pulled off her panties!

Defensively but provocatively, Atty drew up her knees onto her body and spread legs wide apart!

"Don't you dare rape me!" she said provocatively! Rising to the challenge, however, Bill jumped onto the bed, first gave her a nice kiss, and then mounting her he proceeded to "rape" her! It wasn't long before they had an orgasm!

Then Bill's lowered his head between Atty's breasts, and they laid there for a long time.

As evening approached the lovers arose, got dressed, and went over to the main house. Susanna and Juliana had returned, and the four sat on the veranda with drinks. The sisters laughed about Atty's father tantrum, and almost catching Bill in bed with his daughter. Even Bill laughed about even though the whole thing was embarrassing for him.

The four of them had dinner together and spent some time with coffee and brandy, or tea. Then Atty and Bill retired to the guest house, where she stripped him naked, but then allowed him to remove her dress only! Clad only in her bra and panties, she made Bill kneel on the floor in front of her, but with his hands held behind him! Then she unfastened her brassiere and cast it aside, letting her breasts flop almost in his face!

Laughingly she began to whip Bill's face with her breasts, back and forth! Then she rammed one breast and then another into his mouth, while he of course sucked on one nipple and then other!

Atty then made Bill grab hold of her panties in his mouth and forced him to pull them all the way down with his teeth, and off over her high heels! It was awkward for him to remove the garment just with his mouth while at the same time holding his hands behind him!

Bill then picked her up bodily and carried over into the bed, heels and all! Then very slowly he positioned himself on top of her, and when she responded he inserted his hardened organ into her body! Then he proceeded to make love to her in the normal way!

They slept cuddling each other, and then Atty woke him up in the morning as she normally did by lying on top of his naked body! Then she insured his manhood was hard, and taking it in her body, she made love to him until she finally drained his body of its sexual juices! Afterwards they lay of the bed together!

Their romantic slumber, however, was interrupted by some explosions off in the distance! Bill thought that they sounded like bombs and he quickly jumped out of bed! He raced naked to the balcony of the guest house, and was shocked when he heard the low roar of airplanes down near the harbor and explosions in the adjacent airport!

"My God," Bill explained loudly, "the Japanese are bombing Surabaya!" He then quickly got dressed, and used Atty's car and driver to take him down to the base!

22

It was February 3rd and by the time Bill arrived at the base the Japanese planes had left. There was no sign of damage on the naval facilities, and he was informed that the bombing and strafing runs occurred instead on the adjacent air field, and that they had done considerable damage!

Bill was surprised, however, to see a number of Allied cruisers standing out in the bay. He quickly identified the heavy cruiser *Houston* as well as the light cruiser *Marblehead*, and the Dutch light cruiser *De Ruyter*. Also there were four Dutch destroyers at anchor. None of the ships appeared to have been a target for the bombers, but Bill knew that their presence indicated that something was up.

When Bill got to his ship he was told that there was a skippers' meeting in the Task Force headquarters. Luckily he got there just in time, although Henry was already there as the Pope's acting superior officer when the meeting was summoned. Bill asked him to stay for the meeting anyway.

The Dutch Admiral Karel Doorman was introduced to the Americans as the commanding officer of the new proposed naval operation. Bill was amused that this was the same admiral who accompanied Atty's father when they boarded his ship.

The officers were advised that a Japanese force appeared to heading down the Makassar Straits toward the big city of Makassar. The ABDA Command had approved the recommendation of the Dutch Admiral Conrad Helfrich, the senior Dutch admiral in the East Indies, to launch another night attack on the Japanese force similar to the successful Balikpapan attack. Admiral Doorman would lead the force of three cruisers and eight destroyers in his flagship *De Ruyter*. Apparently, the enemy had a sizable navel fighting force as well as transports for the invading troops.

The main problem with the combined Dutch and America task force was that the two navies did not have a common signaling system. And it was too late to coordinate the two systems on the spur of the moment. Additionally, while most Dutch officers spoke English, there was still a problem with the language barrier.

That night the ships departed Surabaya and reassembled at an island off of the most eastern part of Java. The force received a confirmation of the report that the Japanese force invasion force was in the Makassar Strait heading south toward the city of Makassar.

Since the distance to the estimated location of the enemy was sufficiently far, the fleet had to travel part of the way in daylight in order to be able to launch a night attack. That was similar to the previous Balikpapan operation.

Correspondingly, the fleet began to move out that morning and head out into the Java Sea to meet the Japanese force somewhere in the Makassar Strait before it reached the city of Makassar itself. The three cruisers made up the center of the task force with Admiral Doorman's flagship *De Ruyter,* followed by the *Houston*, and then the *Marblehead*. The four

Dutch destroyers flanked the port side with the four destroyers of Division 59, Bill's division, on the starboard side.

It was almost ten o'clock in the morning when suddenly Japanese planes were sighted to the east of the fleet. The Allied ships spread out to prepare maneuvering room for them to take evasive action against the aircraft.

From his vantage point on the bridge of the *Pope*, Bill could see the first wave of bombers concentrating on the *Marblehead,* but they widely missed their target. The second wave, however, managed two hits on the *Marblehead* plus one damaging near miss. He later heard that the hits had killed fifteen men. Meanwhile, the damage caused the ship to lose control of steerage and it had to improvise.

Meanwhile, Bill could see that the bombers were also attacking the *Houston.* There were unsuccessful on most attempts to bomb the ship. On the last run, however, a bomb hit the deck near the after gun, immobilizing it and killing forty-eight crew members, as Bill learned later. At the same time, however, the *De Ruyter* managed to evade most of the attacks and suffered only minor damage.

It obviously was foolish to continue the strike force without air protection. Two of the cruisers were now damaged, one seriously. During the Balikpapan operation the Japanese did not control the skies so the Americans could readily cross the open seas during daylight hours without fear of an aircraft attack.

Realizing this, about one o'clock in the afternoon Admiral Doorman ordered the fleet to return to Java. The *De Ruyter* and the Dutch destroyers headed west toward Tanjung-Priok, while the Americans headed south to the Lessor Sunda Islands. The *Houston* went ahead while the four destroyers escorted the badly crippled *Marblehead.* They passed though the Lombok Strait into the Indian Ocean and then turned west to Tjilatjap on the south coast of Java.

Both cruisers arrived in Tjilatjap to get medical attention for their wounded, to bury their dead, and to get needed repairs. The Marblehead, however, was so badly damaged that eventually it had to return to the States. Bill did not want to go ashore since Tjilatjap was kind of a messy town, unlike the pretty towns of Surabaya or Makassar.

There was a lot of shipping stacked up in the harbor of Tjilatjap waiting for an escort to Australia. Phil's four destroyers were ordered to accompany them to Darwin. The convoy headed east into the Timor Sea and reached Darwin after two days. The destroyers then returned to Surabaya two days later.

.

23

Bill arrived back in Surabaya on February 9th. The Japanese had bombed Surabaya, including the navy yard as well, every day since he left, but the destroyers' wharves were hidden away and protected by camouflage, and weren't touched. But he was told that the Japanese had actually bombed the downtown of the city for the first time that morning.

Bill also learned that the Japanese had already taken Makassar, as well as Banjarmasin in Borneo. That meant that all of the Celebes and Borneo were now in Japanese hands. This allowed them to freely penetrate the Java Sea, as attested by their aircraft bombing of the Allied ships, and undoubtedly they had ships prowling there as well. Even Java was now being bombed by their planes.

Bill called Atty as soon as he could and arranged to meet her that night. As scheduled she picked him up with her car and driver. After hugs and kisses they drove back to the House.

When they were together with Susanna and Juliana, Bill emphasized that the girls must make arrangements now to leave Java as soon as possible. Undoubtedly the Japanese would be coming here eventually and it was imperative that all Dutch nationals get out as quickly as they can.

The girls generally agreed, and stated that all the dependents were already being flown to Australia, but those in Batavia had first priority because of their large numbers. They hoped to be able to leave within a couple of weeks. Bill worried that that may not be soon enough.

The four of them had a nice dinner together and discussed their plans after leaving the East Indies. Afterwards, they had pleasantries before retiring. Once alone with Atty in the guest house Bill got her to agree to make preparations for a quick departure whenever they are allowed to leave. Since, undoubtedly, they would only be allowed one suitcase on the plane on their departure, Bill told her to keep one packed ready to go at any time just in case.

Then they undressed with little sex games, and then made love on the bed in the normal manner! In the morning, Atty woke Bill up in her usual way, and served him breakfast in bed!

Then Bill got dressed and Atty drove him down to the base. As soon as he arrived aboard the *Pope*, he was notified that he was to report to the Task Force headquarters. Expecting something important he rushed over there as quickly as he could.

Bill was directed to the office of one of Admiral Glassford's senior staff officers. The latter informed Bill that a complaint about him had come down through the Dutch Naval channels. The Dutch insisted that Bill be prohibited from leaving the base except on official duties!

Bill insisted that the prohibition was absurd and should be discounted. While the officer agreed that it was a silly order, it indeed was an order that came from the highest Navy levels and must be obeyed. Bill tried to argue the issue, but he was told sternly that the order had to be obeyed -- "the matter was closed"!

Bill, of course, knew that Atty's father was the one behind the restriction just to keep him from his daughter. It was ridiculous, but funny. He then went to the Squadron headquarters and called Atty, telling her about his restriction. She too thought it was ridiculous – but funny. But she said that she would work something out.

Later that afternoon a messenger came from the base clinic that he must report there. When Bill inquired the reason, he was told that he was missing one of his required shots. He wondered about this since as far as he could recollect he was up to date on all his inoculations. But with the Navy being what it was he felt he better go and see.

When Bill arrived at the clinic he was ushered into an exam room. Then a local male orderly told him that he must first take off all his clothes.

"What do mean take off my clothes just for a shot!" Bill replied angrily! "Who in the world required that?"

"The nurse did, sir!" the boy responded.

"What nurse?" Bill demanded heatedly!

"This nurse!" a familiar female voice interjected!

"What …?" Bill muttered as he whirled around!

He was startled to see Atty standing there dressed in a nurse's uniform! A big smile spread over her face.

"Nurse Vanderpan requires that you take off all your clothes!" she said mischievously!

Then she signaled for the boy to leave, and locked the door behinds him!

"Now do what you're told, sailor!" Atty continued. "Strip!"

Under the present circumstances Bill very willingly undressed in front of the "nurse", and then as directed he lay down on the examination table without hesitation. Then Atty came over next to him on the table and made a very professional "examination" of his male sexual organ!

Without saying a word, Atty proceeded to unzip her dress, let it drop, and stepped out of it! Then she unfastened her bra and cast it aside, allowing her breasts to pop into view! Finally she pulled down her panties and took the garment off her feet! Needless to say, Bill greatly enjoyed the "striptease" she performed in front of him while he watched!

Naked except for her heels, Atty climbed up onto the examination table and she straddled over Bill's naked body! Leaning over his head she laughingly dangled her breasts in his face and whipped them back and forth! Each time Bill tied to grasp one of her nipples in his mouth, she playfully pulled it away! But then finally she let him suck one nipple after the other!

Shifting her position, Atty grasped Bill's hardened organ in her hand and rubbed it against her female sex organ! Then she inserted it fully, and lying flat on his body she proceeded to "rape" him as hard as she could!

Bill greatly enjoyed being "raped" by a beautiful and sexy woman, but he could only "last" so long! Atty kept gyrating her pelvis without pause, and then she drained the patient of his sexual juices into her body!

Afterwards, both of them slowly got dressed amid hugs and kisses!

"Thank you, nurse," Bill exclaimed.

"You're welcome, sailor," Atty responded with a smile. "Come back tomorrow for another shot!"

Indeed, after the morning bombing by the Japanese, Bill returned the next day. Then he received similar treatment as before. The patient lay naked on the examination table, the naked nurse took his sexual juices in her body!

This time, however, Bill was able to linger awhile before going back to his ship. They had a late lunch together and were able to sit on the veranda of the hospital and talk and enjoy the scenery. For the time being, they purposely ignored the horrible war events that were closing in upon them.

On the third day something slightly different happened. After the daily bombing Bill came to the clinic as scheduled. He went into the same exam room and proceeded to undress while waiting for Atty to come. The door soon opened and the nurse entered – but it wasn't Atty!

Instead, it was a prudish elderly nurse! When she saw Bill standing there completely naked, she screamed and immediately rushed out of the room! Bill, in shock, tried to cover his private parts! Then he grabbed for some of his clothes!

Shortly afterwards, Atty walked into the room and she was laughing hard! She closed and locked the door behind her!

"You naughty boy!" Atty declared still laughing. "You scared the poor old lady half to death!" Then she walked up to Bill to give him a kiss and at the same time grabbed his male organ and yanked on it!

She pushed Bill to the examination table and made him lie down on it! Atty then made him to spread and arms above his head and his legs wide apart. She ordered him to remain in that position while she punished him for frightening the poor elderly nurse.

Atty proceeded to strip herself as usual in front of Bill, which made Bill's male member to harden into an erection! But instead of jumping on top of him as before, she drew the belt of his pants and told to him to take his punishment like a man!

She then proceeded to whip his naked body with the leather belt! Despite being whipped, the sight of Atty's naked female body in motion and her breasts flopping all around was so exciting that he really enjoyed being "punished"! Realizing this she finally stopped whipping him!

“Oh, you’re such a naughty boy!” Atty insisted as she instead hugged and kissed Bill. Then she swung herself up and on top of his naked body, and teased him with her big breasts again! After allowing him to suck each nipple, she then took his male member into her body and proceeded to “rape” him!

Afterwards, they had a lunch and relaxed on the veranda before Bill had to return to his ship!

24

The next morning was February 13th, and the *Pope* and the rest of the destroyer division had convoy duty again. The Java Sea was no longer safe from Japanese air attacks, and as many commercial shipping as possible had been directed to clear out Surabaya and Tanjung-Priok. These were the only two big ports on the north coast of Java,

Destroyer Division 59 was to escort those ships that were ready to leave Surabaya. They passed through the Bali Strait into the Indian Ocean and then headed toward Darwin. Passing from the Indian Ocean to the Timor Sea, the convoy reached Darwin two days later. After a layover, the destroyers then headed home.

By the time they arrived back in Surabaya on February 18th the situation for the Allies had continued to deteriorate. On one hand, Admiral Hart, the commander of the "deactivated" Asiatic Fleet had been recalled back to the States. That cleared up the confusion of leadership as all the American ships were now definitely in the Southwest Pacific Fleet commanded by Admiral Glassford.

With the departure of Admiral Hart, however, the overall commander of the Allied naval forces passed to the Dutch Admiral Conrad Helfrich. Admiral Glassford, nevertheless, still controlled the American ships. Admiral Hart had recommended that all Allies warships should evacuate the Java Sea and withdraw to Australia since the Japanese now controlled the air and their navy would soon overwhelm Java Sea. Admiral Helfrich, however, demanded that the Allied ships remain on the northern side of Java to defend it against an expected Japanese invasion.

On the other hand, the Japanese finally conquered the British colony of Singapore, only some six hundred miles from Batavia. The overall commander of the American, British, Dutch, and Australian combined command (ABDA), British Field Marshall Sir Archibald Wavell, thereafter was transferred to India and his position in ABDA was taken over by the Dutch Admiral Helfrich.

Even worst was the fact the fact that the Japanese army landed on the island of Sumatra just northwest of Java. They captured Palembang, only just two hundred and fifty miles away Batavia.

Meanwhile, Surabaya, at the opposite end of Java from Batavia, was suffering from the almost daily bombing raids. The airport was largely destroyed and the naval facilities were heavily damaged. While the destroyer wharves at the remote and camouflaged part of the base were untouched, many of the wharves, buildings, and facilities were destroyed. The clinic where Atty and Bill had recently made love was still there, but the hospital was slightly damaged.

Downtown Surabaya had also suffered, particularly along the waterfront. Many shops were shutting down, and lots of the Javanese people were returning to their rural villages. The Chinese-Indonesians, however, had to remain at their shops as they had no other places to go.

The residential areas were not bombed, but some of the fancier houses and mansions, mainly owned by the Dutch government, corporations, or individuals, were being boarded up as their occupants began leaving the colony as fast as they could.

Bill called Atty as soon as possible, but Juliana told him that Atty had gone to Batavia to help her parents. He asked whether she would be returning to Surabaya and Juli didn't think so. She thought that maybe Atty would be flying out to Australia with her parents.

Then Bill asked about her and Susanna's status, and she responded that their names were in a long queue for evacuation. Bill called Atty's phone in Batavia, but it had been disconnected. Then he tried her at her Government House, but he was told that she no longer worked there.

Bill was very concerned about Atty! Luckily, apparently she had managed to leave the Dutch East Indies. But he had missed her departure and would not see her again – maybe never! He was quite sad and depressed!

But Bill had other things to think about. It was reported that a small force of Japanese were attacking the island of Bali just east of Java. Indeed, it was only two hundred miles away from Surabaya. Admiral Helfrich ordered that action be taken to stop the invasion.

Accordingly, Admiral Doorman ordered that all available ships and planes converge to attack the invasion force, which was in the Badung Strait on the east side of the island of Bali.

Two submarines had already engaged the enemy that day, February 18th, but had been driven off. Then later in the day some American planes damaged one transport, but by that time the Japanese had already landed on the island.

The next day, two of Phil's destroyers, Al's *John D. Ford* and Bill's *Pope*, together with the Dutch destroyer *Piet Heim* escorting two Dutch light cruisers, the *De Ruyter* and the *Java*, all headed to Badung Strait. At about ten o'clock that night they sighted the remaining Japanese force of some four destroyers and two transports.

Bill watched from the bridge of the *Pope* as the Dutch cruisers opened fire on the Japanese. No damage was seen, and the cruisers sailed off in the darkness, and let the destroyers use their torpedoes.

Bill and the other two Allied destroyers fired their torpedoes at long distance, and apparently the Japanese destroyer also fired their torpedoes. Indeed, Bill was shocked to see a large explosion on the Dutch destroyer *Piet Hein*, which caused it to sink almost immediately.

The *John D. Ford* and the *Pope* closed in and engaged the four Japanese destroyers in gunfire. Bill was able to see an explosion on one of the Japanese destroyers but he did not know which of the two American ships had made the hit. But then the *Pope* received a near miss that buckled the hull and caused an engine problem. Outnumbered two to one, and with the *Pope* being damaged, Phil directed that the two Americans ships should retire. The Japanese destroyers did not pursue.

But Bill later learned that another group of Allied ships, including the Dutch light cruiser *Tromp* and another four American destroyers arrived in Badung Strait in the morning about three hours later. They managed to damage three of the Japanese destroyers, one badly enough that it had to be towed away. But the *Tromp* was also severely damaged as well.

Then yet another third group, seven torpedo boats, arrived later that morning, but by then the Japanese ships had retired northward. Nevertheless, the Japanese were already on the island and had encountered no resistance on Bali as they easily took over its airpstrip.

Meanwhile, Bill in the *Pope* limped back to Surabaya, escorted by Phil and Al in the *John D. Ford*. They reached the base late at night on February 20th.

The next day Bill learned more horrible news. On February 19th, the same day as the Badung Strait naval battle, the Japanese conducted a bombing raid on Darwin, which devastated its port facilities. This was the first Japanese attack on Australia itself.

Then the next day the Japanese invaded Timor in the eastern part on the Dutch East Indies. The Japanese net was now slowly closing in upon the last remaining bastion of the Dutch colony, the densely populated island of Java.

It was now February 21st and Bill had to care for his ship. The remaining facilities in the Navy Yard for repair work were meager, but Henry was a mechanical engineer, and he was very good at improvising. He left the repair of the ship in his hands, which he estimated to take about a week. At the same time Bill concentrated more on supplying the ship with munitions and general provisions.

As the days passed by Bill checked with Juliana or Susanna whether they had heard any news about Atty, but they hadn't. He was extremely worried about her and hoped that she and her family had been able to get out of Batavia by now. But on the other hand, Bill was greatly saddened to have not been able to see before her departure.

The sisters invited Bill up to the house once, and with permission he brought Phil and Henry along to give them a needed break. The five of them had drinks on the veranda overlooking the harbor, which still looked beautiful despite the war damage, particularly in the early evening. Then they had a nice leisurely dinner with wine followed by coffee and brandy and tea! Bill and Henry then went back to the base and their quarters, and Phil came later!

25

It was four days later on February 25th, and Bill just happened to be in the facility that now served as the Squadron headquarters later in the day, when a clerk advised him that there was a call for him. The latter told him that it was a female. His spirits surged as he hoped that it was one of the sisters with some news about Atty! He dashed to the phone and picked up the receiver.

"Hello, Admiral Darling!" came the sweet voice of Atty herself. Bill was overwhelmed with joy! She had not departed to Australia.

"No, darling," she happily answered his question as to her whereabouts! "I am here in Surabaya waiting for my sailor darling to come up to the house and make love to me!"

Bill rushed back to the ship to advise Henry where he was going and then rushed to the front gate to greet Atty. When she arrived Atty gave Bill a hug and a kiss, and then pulled him into the car with her! They kissed again, but then she hugged him and broke down in tears.

"What's the matter, darling?" Bill asked, as he had never seen her cry before.

"It's my parents," Atty sobbed! Bill held her tightly and tried to calm her as best as he could, not knowing the reason for her tears. Finally, her sobbing subsided and she was able to talk.

“My mother had a stroke!” Atty sniffled, “and she is in the hospital near death. That is why I went back to Batavia.”

“Oh my dear!” Bill consoled Atty, remembering her mother when he first met her, and Atty, on the outskirts of Olongapo soon after his arrived in the Philippines.

“And my father won’t leave her!” Atty continued. “He insists on staying with her to the end!” She burst out sobbing again.

As they rode up to her house, Bill held Atty tightly and kissed him passionately all the way up the hill. It had been almost two weeks since they were last together – and a lot had changed since then.

When they entered the house Bill was surprised by how busy the sisters were in arranging things and by the collection of boxes sitting around. He inquired on what was happening.

“Didn’t she tell you?” Juliana asked excitedly! When Bill’s looks pleaded ignorance, she quickly continued. “Atty arranged our departure while she was in Batavia. We are confirmed to be flying out tomorrow night – all three of us!”

Bill was elated they were getting out of harm’s way, but of course saddened that his love was leaving – permanently. Atty apologized for not telling him right away, but she was so glad to see him and was so upset about her parents.

Susanna confirmed that the three of them would be leaving Surabaya the next night. She explained that they would be letting all the servants go, most of who would be returning to their villages. The house itself belonged to the Dutch government, and the government had already hired someone to close up the building. Meanwhile, since each passenger was allowed only one suitcase, the girls had been spending a lot of time deciding what to take and what to leave behind.

But for now, they agreed that the four of them were going to have a grand going-away party that night among themselves. First they had drinks on the veranda as the sun went down. Then the sisters had arranged with the servants to prepare a special last dinner for them. There was a lot of food served with wine, followed with coffee, tea, and brandy. They all had brandy, including Atty who normally did not drink much at all.

Juli in particular drank a lot. She even started flirting with Bill while Sue, her older sister, scolded her. But then Juli jumped into Bill's lap, threw her arms around his neck, and kissed him passionate. Before Bill could really react, Atty was up in arms and pulled Juli away roughly. Both Atty and Sue railed at Juli in Dutch. Finally, things settled down and soon everyone was laughing again.

Finally it was time for bed, and Bill and Atty went to the guest house so that they could have a loving reunion – and farewell!

Indeed, they embraced and kissed as they started undressing each other! While Atty pulled off his shirt, dropped his pants, and pulled down his shorts, Bill unzipped and pulled down her dress!

He unfastened Atty's brassiere and fondled her breasts! Then Bill pressed his naked body against her to feel her naked breasts against his chests and her panties against his naked erected organ. As he lowered himself, he sucked on each of her nipples, and then pulled down her panties!

Bill then picked up Atty bodily and carried her over to the bed and laid her flat on her back! He fondled her big breasts again, and sucked on her nipples! Then he rubbed his naked male body against her naked female body! Finally, he entered her body with his manhood and proceeded to make love to her!

Bill tried to make love slowly but since it been almost two weeks since they were in bed together previously, it was hard for him to control his physical desires! Indeed, even Atty herself gyrated her pelvis vigorously which reduced Bill's resistance! He could not hold back very long, and soon they reached a reached a climax and had a sexual orgasm!

Then they cuddled naked and sleep for the night.

But early in the morning, Atty crawled on top of Bill and laughingly proceeded to make love to him! Needless to say, he quite enjoyed it!

Bill got dressed and was driven down to base by the driver. He had things to do there and on the ship, including holding out for any bombing run. Henry advised him that the repair work on the Pope was almost complete and should be ready by late the next day.

Bill advised Henry that the girls were leaving that evening. When the car came to pick up Bill, Henry went with him as far as the front gate to say farewell to Atty. She gave Henry a hug and a kiss and wished him well. Then she pulled Bill into the car with her and together they rode back up to the house.

"Have you had your lunch?" Atty asked mischievously! When he acknowledged that he had not, she cocked her finger at him and beckoned him back to the guest house! They stripped, embraced, and kissed. Atty then lay back on the bed, pulled her knees way up and far apart!

Dutifully, Bill entered her and made love to her!

Then the lovers laid back and as they rested Atty made Bill promise that he would also be coming to Australia as well. Then they napped for most of the rest of the afternoon.

Dressed and back in the main house, Bill could see that the girls had more or less made the final preparations! All the servants had already left, and the Chinese-Indonesian caretakers were now at the house beginning to close it up as the girls were departing. All four of them had a final farewell drink, and ate some sandwiches that had been prepared for them.

Then the girls made the last hurried adjustments to their luggage. They were in a panic as they kept changing their minds to what to bring and what to leave behind. But finally they were ready to go!

The car transported them to the airport, or what was left of it after being repeatedly bombed by the Japanese. There were no terminals, no hangers, and no planes left. The plane that was going to take them to Australia would be flying in from Batavia. Fortunately, there was enough runway left to allow the plane to land and take off again.

After turning their luggage over to the Javanese attendant they all waited in the car until dusk and the arrival of the plane. Susanne and Juliana, both who had spent several years in the Dutch East Indies, were sad in leaving Java, but understandably glad they were leaving at this time. They hoped to be able to come back after the war. Atty was sad leaving her sick mother and her father behind – and, of course, her lover!

Bill tried to commiserate with all of them. He told them that the war would not last too long and that they could all get together again. Meanwhile, the girls could begin a new life in Australia. All three girls tried to be as optimistic as possible as the present circumstances allowed them.

The sun finally set and darkness set up. Their plane would now be leaving Batavia, Bill assured them, and then several hours later they finally heard the approaching aircraft. The two sisters exited the car while Atty and Bill stayed for one last embrace and kiss. It was then that Atty made a starling announcement!

"Darling, I am pregnant!" she said!

"What … ?" Bill stammered.

"Yes, Darling, I am carrying your child." Atty stated without hesitation. And then she leaned to him and kissed him.

"How can you be so sure?" Bill asked in wonderment.

"A woman knows these things," Atty assured him. "And I had the feeling that I conceived when we made love up at Puncak Pass!"

"Oh, my goodness," Bill exclaimed, "I am going to be a father – again!" Then he embraced and kissed her!

"Now you have to come to Australia!" Atty demanded.

"I promise to get there, one way or another" Bill insisted, "I want to see the birth of my child!"

Bill wanted to talk more about Atty's pregnancy, but they were interrupted by calls from the girls. Their plane had landed and it was pulling up to gate. Atty and Bill quickly walked arm in arm out to the departure gate where the girls and others passengers were waiting. They hugged each other as the aircraft pulled up to gate.

They had to wait until the attendant loaded the luggage on the plane. Then Bill escorted them all the girls to the bottom of the stairs. Sue and Juli each gave him a hug and kiss. Juli reminded him that if he got tired of the old hag, pointing to Atty, she was still available. Then the two sisters boarded the plane.

Atty then embraced Bill and gave him a long, long, long farewell kiss! Sue and Juli were already on the plane, and they called on Atty to hurry up. Tearfully, she ascended the stairway, turned to wave to Bill, and then disappeared. The door was shut and the engines were revived up, as Bill was pulled back to the gate.

He stood watching as the plane taxied back out onto the runway. His heart sank as the plane turned and roared down the runway. He felt miserable. Despite what he said earlier he really had the feeling that he probably would never see Atty again. He lingered to watch the lights of the plane as it disappeared into the night, and the sound faded away. Then all was silent!

“Good-bye, my love!” barely issued from Bill’s mouth!

26

When Bill returned to the base that night he was surprised to see the lights of different ships slipping into the harbor. Something big was afoot, and Bill had a restless night – both with the departure of Atty and with the arrival of so many ships indicating another operation was at hand.

The next morning, February 27th, Bill clearly made out the various cruisers, including two heavy cruisers, the *Houston* and the British *Exeter*, and three light cruisers, including the Dutch *De Ruyter* and *Java*, and the Australian *Perth*, as well as three British and two Dutch destroyers. That was in addition to the five American destroyers already in the port. Obviously, they had been assembled for a specific purpose.

Bill soon found out at a meeting held that morning for the skippers of all the ships. A large Japanese invasion transport force, escorted by a big force of warships, had been sighted coming down Makassar Strait. This undoubtedly was an invasion force aimed on landing on Java itself.

Admiral Helfrich, the Dutch commanding officer of ABDA, was determined to attack this invasion force before it could reach Java. Therefore he scraped together a naval force of the four countries under the ABDA Command from all available vessels in the Java Sea.

Unfortunately, the communication and coordination between the four navies, particularly with the Dutch ships, was poor. In addition, the Japanese ships were very modern while the

Allies ships were of an older vintage. And the *Houston's* after gun turret had been knocked out of action.

The Allied fleet sailed out of Surabaya later that morning and headed northeast across the Java Sea. Phil led Destroyer Division 59 with them but without the *Pope*, which was still under repair. Phil picked up another destroyer so that there were four of them including his flagship the *John D. Ford* commanded by Bill's friend Al, the *Alden*, the *John D. Edwards*, and the *Paul Jones,* the latter being commanded by Bill's friend Dick Rogers.

The *Pope* actually was ready for action later that afternoon, long after the task force had left. Bill was ordered to stand by for the time being.

Meanwhile, he listened intently to the reports as they came to what later would be referred to as the "Battle of Java Sea".

About four o'clock in the afternoon a report was received that the Japanese fleet had been sighted and that gunfire was being exchanged, but without much happening. Then came the report that a Japanese heavy cruiser had been badly damaged and withdrew from the battle. Then an enemy light cruiser was hit and withdrew. The Japanese attempted a destroyer torpedo attack but were driven off by cruiser gunfire.

But then the *Houston* and the Dutch light cruiser *Java* were both hit, but luckily with only minor damage. About five-thirty, however, the *Exeter* received a serious hit and turned away from the battle. The other Allied ships turning to cover it with a smoke screen. Then the Dutch destroyer *Kortenaer* was hit by a torpedo and sunk very quickly.

Meanwhile, Japanese destroyers were closing in to attack the damaged *Exeter* and the three British destroyers responded to in a counterattack. One of them, the *Electra*, was hit by cruiser fire and soon also was sunk, but the *Exeter* was saved. It was ordered back to Surabaya, escorted by the Dutch destroyer *Witte De With*.

With the *Pope* now ready for action, Bill was ordered to sail out and assist the *Witte De With* in escorting the *Exeter* back to Surabaya. He went out and met the two ships, and all three of them returned to the port without any further incident.

Meanwhile, as the Allies reformed and began to withdraw from the action, the *Houston* managed to sink a Japanese destroyer, and then apparently an enemy cruiser. Meanwhile, due to confused signals from Admiral Doorman, the four American destroyers under Phil thought they were ordered to attack some new enemy cruisers reported to be on the scene. Under heavy fire they came as close as they dared and fired all their torpedoes. Then with their torpedoes expended they too headed back to Surabaya. While the torpedoes made no hits, they forced the Japanese to turn away and the battle was ended, temporarily at least.

The Allied fleet was now limited to the four cruisers and two British destroyers. Admiral Doorman, in accordance to his orders, was determined to reach and attack the Japanese invasion transports. After sunset the fleet turned northward again, and at about seven-thirty at night enemy warships were spotted. The fleet turned east to avoid them, but soon the Japanese lit the skies with flares. After they died off, Admiral Doorman turned the fleet south toward Java, and then west along the coast still hoping to reach the invasion transports.

Then the British destroyer *Jupiter* was "torpedoed" [actually it hit a mine] and had to be left behind. Soon the fleet encountered the survivors of the *Kortenaer* in the water, and the British destroyer *Encounter* was directed to pick them up and take them back to Surabaya.

The fleet, now limited to just four cruisers, continued onward and encountered a series of water-borne flares as if the Japanese were marking their path. But then the flares disappeared. At about eleven o'clock at night two cruisers were sighted, shots were fired, but then the Japanese disappeared in the darkness.

Then about midnight the Dutch cruiser *Java* was hit by an explosion from an unknown source, and soon afterwards Admiral Doorman's flagship *De Ruyter* was hit by a torpedo. Both ships soon sank, and the admiral went down with them.

The *Houston* and the Australian *Perth*, the last ships of the task force, were ordered to retire to Batavia, and they soon were able to escape the scene. They arrived at Tanjung-Priok early in the morning.

Back in Surabaya, meanwhile, Bill was waiting with the damaged *Exeter* and the Dutch destroyer escort *Witte De With*. Then he saw Phil's four destroyers return from the battle as well some two hours later, their torpedoes already expended. As soon as possible he met with Phil, Al, and the other skippers and talked about the battle. Then later that night the British destroyer *Encounter* arrived with the survivors from the Dutch destroyer *Kortenaer.*

At any rate, they all tried to get a good night's sleep for their unknown fate on the morrow. Bill, meanwhile, kept hoping that Atty's plane had made it all right to Perth.

27

It was February 28th the next morning, and the captains of the surviving ships met to determine their next course of action. Admiral Helfrich ordered that all remaining warships should leave the Dutch East Indies for Australia that very night, and all other personnel to leave as best as they could.

In Tanjung-Priok, the remaining warships were the cruisers the *Houston*, and the *Perth*. They were directed to escape through the Sunda Strait that lay between Java and Sumatra that night. Intelligence seemed to indicate that there were no Japanese ships in that area that would prevent their escape.

The port of Tjilatjap, on the south coast of Java, had many ships, including the American destroyers *Pillsbury* and *Parrott*. But by now Japanese ships had also entered the Indian Ocean looking for any stray Allied ships. Many of these ships left Tjilatjap that night, each going independently to avoid the enemy. But some of these ships were sunk, one of them being the *Pillsbury*.

In Surabaya, The remaining warships included the damaged heavy cruiser *Exeter* and seven destroyers. The British heavy cruiser *Exeter* was famous for its role in sinking the German battleship *Admiral Graf Spee* in the Battle of River Plate in South America. But it was badly damaged from yesterday's battle with the Japanese in the Java Sea.

The destroyers included Phil's Destroyer Division's *John D. Ford* commanded by Bill's friend Al, the *Alden*, the *John D. Edwards*, and the *Paul Jones*. But they had all expended all their torpedoes. It also included Bill's *Pope* that was still fully armed.

Another American destroyer was the *Steward* that had been badly damaged in a separate action earlier off of Sumatra and had to be left behind. The Dutch destroyer *Witte De With* had mechanical difficulties and also had to be remain behind in Surabaya. And the last destroyer was the British *Encounter*.

The safest and fastest escape route for these remaining ships to leave from Surabaya was to sail directly east of the port through the Madura Strait and then down the Bali Strait to the Indian Ocean and onward to Australia. The Madura Strait, however, was considered too shallow for a big ship like the heavy cruiser *Exeter* and it was determined that the safest route for it was through the Sunda Strait at the other end of Java, similar to that for the *Houston* and *Perth*. The *Encounter* and the *Pope*, both still fully armed with torpedoes, were directed to escort it. Phil's four destroyers, on the other hand, would take the shorter Madura and Bali Straits route.

During the day repairs were made on the *Exeter* to allow it to permit a speed of about twenty-three knots. And every ship made preparations to leave Surabaya permanently. The remaining naval facilities would be destroyed by the Dutch before the Japanese arrived. Everyone had a good rest and a good meal during the day before the attempted escapes that night. Bill said goodbye to his fellow American skippers.

As soon as darkness settled in, the four American destroyers, including the *John D. Ford*, the *Alden*, the *John D. Edwards*, and the *Paul Jones,* headed east through the Madura Strait and then south down through the Bali Straits.

About the same time the *Exeter*, the *Encounte*r, and the *Pope* entered the Java Sea and headed west along the Java coast toward Sunda Strait. Since there was always a possibility of encountering a Japanese warship, Bill remained in the in a little cabin right behind the bridge.

He lay there on the cot contemplating their chances to get out of the Java Sea. Despite what he told Atty, he feared that their chances were slim. All depended on whether they would encounter any Japanese warships. The *Houston* and *Perth* had a better chance since they could reach Sunda Strait that night.

But the *Pope* and British ships would have to spend that night and the next day in the Java Sea before they reached the strait. With the Japanese now basically controlling the Java Sea, undoubtedly Japanese ships and aircrafts would be searching for any stray Allied warships that were still there. It would be extremely lucky if they remained undetected during the whole of the next day.

Pessimistically, Bill's mind automatically shifted that what he was leaving behind. He thought about his three daughters. They were all teenagers now. While technically they had a father, a step-father, Bill sensed that it was not all right with them, especially the eldest one.

And then there was little Billy. Being only four years old, he might more easily recover from his absence. The problem with him was that there was no potential step-father to take his place – or at least not yet. And Bill thought he would suffer growing up with a weird mother and no father. A boy needs a father more than a girl does, or at least that was what Bill felt.

And now there was a fifth child – his child that Atty was carrying. Undoubtedly, Atty could marry Hans as it had already been planned previously. He assumed that Atty and the other two girls made it safely to Perth. Then she and Hans could get married in Australia. But the thought of Hans marrying Atty and being the father of his child disturbed him.

That made his mind switch Atty herself. He began to think about all the wonderful times that had together. He remembered their first meeting near Olongapo in the Philippines, the party at the Dutch Embassy in Manila, the Thanksgiving dinner at Subic Bay, the sightseeing and dinner in Manila, and swimming in Manila Bay. And, of course, he could never forget when they first made love in her house in Manila.

Then there was the bombing of the *Pope* and his session in the hospital. And Atty made love to him there. Thinking about it made him automatically reach for her panties that he kept hidden on his person, and he was thrilled by the nice soft feel of the feminine garment.

And he remembered the shock to find out that she was already engaged to be married when he met her father in Ambon. But he was so delighted to see her again there in Ambon, and make love in the backseat of a car.

In Surabaya, Bill probably broke all sorts on Navy regulations when he flew off to Batavia to search for her. And then they made love in her house in Batavia. But certainly the highlight of that time was their wonderful "honeymoon" at Puncak Pass, and on the slopes of Mount Pangrango.

And finally he thought about all the times they had together in Surabaya. He spent time with her in the guest house, in downtown Surabaya, and in the hospital. And then there was the dinner party and a garden party sponsored by the lovely Dutch girls for the officers of the destroyer division.

Bill finally dozed off a bit with the thoughts of Atty lingering in his mind. But then he was suddenly aroused just before midnight by Ensign Roberts.

"Commander, sir, the *Houston* is in trouble!" Roberts exclaimed in a panic.

Bill rushed into the radio room. From the reports being sent back to the Bandung headquarters the *Houston* and *Perth* had run into a large Japanese invasion force at Bantam Bay just before reaching the Sunda Strait. The invasion force reportedly was being escorted by many cruisers and destroyers.

Bill and the others listened as a furious battle was taking place. The Allied ships were in the middle of the enemy at night, and there was a considerable confusion among the Japanese defenders. But after about an hour of fighting the listeners heard that the two Allied cruisers abandoned ship, and presumably their vessels were soon sunk.

Upon hearing that a large force of Japanese ships were at or around the Sunda Strait, the proposed escape route for the

Exeter and its destroyer escorts, the *Exeter* signaled for the little fleet to turn northward towards Borneo. Perhaps they could better remain undetected near Borneo during the next day, and then try again for the Sunda Strait the next night.

Bill and the rest of the crew were quite upset about the tragic fate of the *Houston* and the *Perth*. The presence of a large Japanese naval force near the Sunda Strait, as well as another similar force at the eastern end of the Java Sea that the Allies encountered the night before greatly reduced their chances of escape. They probably were now trapped in the Japanese controlled Java Sea!

Upon hearing this latest development, hardly anyone could go back to sleep. Bill remained on the bridge now, and as the night passed on his thoughts continued to be of Atty. For sure now he would never see his love again.

At about four o'clock in the morning the *Exeter* signaled that it had sighted a ship to the east. The Allies, still in the darkness of night, turned northwest to avoid any contact.

It was now March 1st and Bill and the crew of the *Pope* had an early breakfast before sunrise, and then Bill was back on the bridge. As the sun rose there was no enemy vessel in sight, and he had a slight hope that they might remain undetected.

But then about seven o'clock the *Exeter* signaled that it had sighted two Japanese cruisers and a destroyer to the east. Since the Allies were still shadowed by the night's darkness, they were able to continue undetected.

The relief of not encountering the enemy ships was soon dispelled, however, by the sighting of a single-engine seaplane that came over the horizon and circled over the ships. It was above gun range, and presumably it was radioing the position of the Allied ships. Then the plane flew away. The *Exeter* then changed course again hoping to mislead the enemy.

But about nine o'clock, however, a destroyer came streaming toward them from the south. The *Exeter* fired at it from extreme range, and the destroyer turned and disappeared.

Shortly afterwards, however, it returned with three more destroyers and two heavy cruisers, all coming at top speed. The Allies turned away from the pursuing Japanese ships, but the Exeter's reduced speed was not capable of outrunning the enemy. By about ten-twenty the Japanese ships, coming from two directions, now came within range of the Allied ships.

While the *Exeter* opening fire on the cruisers, the *Encounter* and the *Pope* rushed forward to meet the fast approaching destroyers and fired upon them. Bill's guns managed to hit one of the enemy destroyers, which withdrew on fire and smoke. The Japanese cruisers, however, were zeroing in on the *Exeter* with close salvos.

In order to give the *Exeter* some relief, Bill turned the *Pope* between it and the enemy cruisers while laying a smoke screen. The *Exeter* and *Encounter* also laid smoke. This caused the Japanese to cease firing and allowed the *Exeter* to change its course. So far the Allied ships seemingly were holding their own against the enemy. But their hope of escape was minimal.

But about eleven o'clock two more Japanese heavy cruisers and three more destroyers joined the battle, and soon the *Exeter* was under heavy fire. Both the *Exeter* and *Pope* fired its torpedoes and one of them hit one of the Japanese cruisers.

But about eleven-thirty the *Exeter* took a serious hit, and it was in flames as it slowed to a standstill. Since the cause of the British cruiser was now hopeless, the *Encounter* and the *Pope* were ordered to run for a nearby rain squall.

Japanese destroyers closed in on the helpless *Exeter* and finished it with torpedoes. The famous British fighting ship was sunk about eleven-forty!

Meanwhile, the Japanese now concentrated on the fleeing destroyers. The *Encounter* could not maintain the speed of the *Pope* or to outrun the enemy. It sailed between the Japanese and the *Pope* and it became the target for the Japanese. It was soon hit by a cruiser shell that caused it to lose all power. The crew abandoned the ship and soon it too was sunk.

The *Pope*, meanwhile, was racing to the nearby rain squall as fast as it could go. Cruiser shells were falling just behind it when Bill reached the squall and the ship disappeared from the Japanese view.

28

The *Pope* was now temporally safe in the rain squall, and Bill turned north toward Borneo again. He quickly figured that their only chance to escape was to reach the Borneo coast and elude the Japanese for the rest of the day. Then he could make a run for the Lombok Strait in the Lesser Sunda Islands and onward to Australia the next night. It was a slim chance, but it appeared the only one available to him.

Meanwhile, Bill and the crew had a chance to relax just a little bit. The rain squall kept the ship hidden for the time being and the *Pope* did not have to dodge Japanese shells. Bill used the time to assess the ship's condition and armament and he arranged a redistribution of the ship's shells.

But it was a very short reprieve! The rain cover only lasted for about ten minutes. Nevertheless, it still shielded the ship from the enemy, and Bill immediately headed into another small shower. But this lasted only a few minutes and then once more the *Pope* was out in the open again.

No enemy ships were sighted and the *Pope* sped on its way northward towards Borneo. Bill grimaced as the *Pope* was the last warship in the old Asiatic Fleet left in the Java Sea! Indeed, it the last warship of the entire Allied fleet that still survived in these waters.

Hopes of reaching Borneo undetected, however, were short-lived when shortly after noon a single-engine seaplane was spotted, which began to follow the *Pope*. Soon it was joined by another plane. Then fifteen minutes later six more planes arrived.

All eight planes then began to make bombing runs on the *Pope*. During most of the runs only one near miss caused some minor damage. Bill made every effort to evade the bombs and was largely successful. On the eleventh run, however, another near miss knocked a big hole in the hull and caused the loss of one engine.

By now the planes had used up all their bombs and everyone was grateful when they flew off. But the *Pope* was in serious trouble.

Indeed, moments later six twin-engine bombers appeared in the sky. Then they too prepared to attack the already stricken ship. The *Pope* was already flooding and steerage was difficult when the bombers made their first attack. Bill, however, managed to evade the bombs just in time.

After the bombers made an unsuccessful second bombing run, Rogers, the damage control officer, reported that the flooding could not be stopped! The *Pope* was settling by the stern! Henry went down to confirm it.

Finally Bill brought the *Pope* to a complete halt and ordered the crew to abandon ship!

The motor launch, lifeboats, and rafts were quickly dispatched down to the water. The well trained crew did not panic as they too made their way off the ship. Bill sent Henry down to organize the crew down below in the water. He made sure everyone found refuge in the launch, the lifeboats, or the rafts or the power launch.

Then Bill directed Worthington, the gunnery officer, and his crew to prepare charges for scuttling the ship. Most everyone made it off the *Pope* all right, and only Bill and a few others were still left.

Bill was shocked, however, to see some of the Japanese bombers sweep low and begin to strafe the men in the water or on rafts. Henry scattered the collection of men, and fortunately it seemed as if most of the shots went wild. It appeared as if nobody was seriously hurt.

Bill was still on the ship when suddenly he saw big explosions erupting in the water all around the *Pope*! He looked up to see two Japanese cruisers closing in fast and they were firing to finish off the poor stricken ship.

Bill was almost in a state of shock as some cruiser shells struck the *Pope*! Then he knew that it was the end! Ironically, at this moment of peril his mind could only think of one thing! Images of Atty flashed through his mind! Then a gigantic explosion hit the bridge! And amidst all the smoke, flames, and flying shrapnel, Bill had only one last though …

"Good-bye, my Love!"

Epilogue

The USS *Pope* sank minutes later on March 1, 1942, at about one o'clock in the afternoon. Most of the crew survived and were picked up by the Japanese and transported to a prisoners of war camp.

The two Japanese invasion forces, one east and one west, landed at four different places on Java, also on March 1st. The Japanese quickly drove the Dutch defenders into the interior. Japanese soldiers captured the cities of Batavia, Surabaya, and Tjilatjap on March 7th. The Dutch surrendered Java and the entire Dutch East Indies to the Japanese on March 8th. All Dutch and other Western nationals were rounded up and were imprisoned in concentration camps. A few Dutch nationals and sympathetic Indonesians were summarily executed! Atty's father was one of them!

On the other hand, the four destroyers of Commander Phil Tower's Destroyer Division 59 had a slight brush with a Japanese ship in the Bali Strait during the previous night, but thereafter they made it safely all the way to Perth, Australia, by March 3rd.

CPSIA information can be obtained at www.ICGtesting.com
Printed in the USA
BVOW070601050112

279828BV00001B/74/P

9 781462 650613